SILVER EAGLE

A RED BRANCH MISSION
BOOK 2

BLAZE WARD

KNOTTED ROAD PRESS

ALSO BY BLAZE WARD

The Science Officer Series

Start with: The Science Officer

The Jessica Keller Chronicles

Start with: Auberon

CS-405 (Command Centurion Kosnett, part of Jessica)

Start with: Queen Anne's Revenge

First Centurion Kosnett (sequel to Jessica)

Start with: Encounter at Vilahana

Additional Alexandria Station Stories

Alexandria Station Collection

Handsome Rob (Alexandria Station Universe)

Start with: Can't Shoot Straight Gang

=====================

Corsac Fox

Start with: Flight of the Corsac Fox

Operation Marrakesh

Start with: Trial by Leviathan

Captain Daring

Start with: Revoked

The Hunter Bureau

Start with: Mirrors

Fairchild

Start with: Fairchild

Last Stand

Start with: Lost Dreams

The Lazarus Alliance

Start with: Escape

Shadow of the Dominion

Start with: Longshot Hypothesis

Star Dragon

Start with: Birth of the Star Dragon

Kincaide's War

Start with: The Eden Package

Star Tribes

Start with: Winterstar

Blaze also writes Action-Adventure Here

PART ONE
HUNTERS

CHAPTER 1

Colonel Gennadi Ivanov Nazarenko was still settling in to his new role, having never expected to live as a spy. Doubly so in the now-hostile West, as the wartime alliance with America and Britain had disintegrated before his very eyes over the last few years.

Gennadi looked up as his office door opened suddenly. Ireland was almost as cold and foggy as Moscow might be this morning, and he had not been expecting company.

Thus, he was doubly surprised when Comrade General Shuysky entered. Even in mufti, the man moved like the Soviet Air Forces General he was. Heavy, with smooth hands. Siberian face from the days of the Golden Horde. Gray hair brushed back.

Gennadi automatically rose, but Shuysky waved him to sit with a broad smile. Yefim, Gennadi's assistant, hovered nervously behind the general in the hallway.

"Coffee," Gennadi tole the young man who had accompanied him from Mother Russia.

Whatever was happening, it could not be good if Comrade General Shuysky had traveled secretly to Ireland to talk.

Yefim nodded and fled. Gennadi stared at the man and waited until two mugs got delivered and the door closed firmly.

They sipped companionably for a moment. The General nodded and scowled.

"At least as good as the best black market coffee we can get in Moscow," he muttered darkly. "And that for the top. Here, the Irish drink it everyday."

"Many sacrifices were needed to save the world, sir," Gennadi replied darkly, stopping himself short of name or rank.

The base he was operating from was populated by Irish Reds with a deep and historic loathing of the English, aggravated by the Civil War a generation ago. *Their* civil war, ousting the English from most of the island after centuries of occupation.

"Call me Zinoviy in public, Gennadi," the man ordered.

Still his boss, even if they were out of uniform, far from home, and hiding from almost everyone.

Gennadi nodded. Waited.

"Have you considered what it means that your Red Branch are coming to be seen as heroes in the West?" Zinoviy asked abruptly.

"They are in a better place to hunt escaped war criminals," Gennadi replied. "And worse, because they cannot operate so much in the shadows. At the same time, I believe that helps Sasha, as long as they believe him to be your enemy. The Jews and the Americans will be his allies in hunting those Nazis who escaped our wrath. Those the Americans haven't themselves hired."

The General nodded and sipped.

"Technology moves rapidly," he continued, apparently happy to start in the middle and hare all over the place, but

Gennadi had served under the man long enough to understand.

They were both GRU. The Main Intelligence Directorate of the Soviet General Staff, though a small department hidden away in one corner, dedicated to hunting down those war criminal Nazis that had escaped justice with the help of the Pope and his damnable Ratlines.

Those the Americans had kidnapped were generally beyond Soviet justice. For now. Nuremberg had left a good accounting of the ones that Stalin's armies hadn't taken for punishment.

A few yet remained.

Gennadi waited as Zinoviy hesitated.

"Technology," he repeated. "How soon until the Nightviper is obsolete?"

Gennadi nodded, understanding.

"The so-called second series of jets is about to be superseded by a third," he replied. "The German ME 262 inspired many imitators, including our own Sukhoi Su-9 and Su-11. The Mikoyan-Gurevich MiG-9 is a good enough aircraft, and entered service last year, but I understand that the new swept-wing Mikoyan-Gurevich MiG-15 is so much better that is yet another revolution in aviation. And hopefully a terrible surprise to our foes when it goes fully into service. I have no doubts that the Americans and British will field equally impressive craft to replace the old Gloster Meteors or Lockheed P-80 Shooting Stars. In South America, there are no aircraft currently good enough to challenge the Nightviper in single combat. Even the German refugee Tank will be hard pressed, starting from nothing."

"However, you have only three pilots," Zinoviy nodded.

"All exceptional, but they can be beaten on pure numbers, as we did to the Nazis."

"Have you found a replacement that we could add?" Gennadi asked.

"I have not," the man shook his head. "Sasha might have to recruit an outsider. Is he up for it?"

"I believe so," Gennadi replied. "He has already carried the weight of the world on his shoulders, keeping the Werewolf Legion from bombing New York City and possibly igniting a war nobody wants."

"Nobody wants," Zinoviy agreed. "We intend to absorb the rest of Europe quietly. Or had. The air armada feeding Berlin all winter seems to have inspired the West to finally push back. And the German public to choose sides. That leaves us with Eastern Europe to digest. After that, I do not know."

"What happens after Stalin?" Gennadi asked, willing to face these things, here in his office in Ireland, far from the Soviets and commissars.

The Generalissimo was in his seventies. And whispers suggested that he was slowing down. If not done, possibly close to the end. Perhaps not there yet, but soon enough that the maneuvering to replace him had begun. That had led to another purge, under the cover of which Gennadi and Zinoviy had recruited the Red Branch and gotten them safely to Ireland, and then Argentina.

"I cannot say, Gennadi," the man acknowledged. "Perhaps Molotov. Perhaps Khrushchev. Perhaps both will be ousted by some as-yet unknown third. The Red Branch must be protected. Expanded. Kept up to date with technology as it advances, so that they can continue to punish those who fled Berlin ahead of us and think that our reach is not long enough."

"This factory can be scaled up to produce more aircraft, Zinoviy," Gennadi nodded. "We have not, as yet, because we already have more planes than pilots, as well as sufficient spare parts stockpiled. And no understanding of what we might build that is better, like the new swept-wing jets. The MiG-15 and whatever else comes. What do we need to build?"

"I cannot say, but part of my mission here is to prepare you for perhaps making this a permanent assignment, Gennadi," the man said sternly. "Red Branch Command, as it is called, must have a manager, even if our Sasha is the actual unit commander. He will need this industry supporting him. Building for him. Money has been quietly set aside and will be made available for you to turn this into a proper facility, along with cover stories hinting at both White Russian investors and secret American operations."

Gennadi could not contain his gasp. He was not an old man, barely forty-seven. It was the injuries from the war that slowed him down. Made him walk with a cane many days. Turned his beard white. Kept him from flying warplanes in combat again.

But to become the proper managing director of Red Branch Command? Permanently remain in Ireland, or wherever the job might take him later?

Heady stuff. But the GRU had prepared him, just as he had set Sasha and the others up for success.

"What else can our spies steal from the British?" Gennadi asked after he settled his stomach. And soul. "Already, they gave us the Nene engine that we have improved for the MiG-15 and the Nightviper. What comes after the de Havilland Venom that became our Nightviper? Are the Americans building better ideas that our spies can steal, as the Werewolf Legion did with their Curtiss-Wright Blackhawks?"

"I shall inquire," Zinoviy nodded. "For now, I need you to send the team to Paraguay. You will need to travel there as soon as possible to brief them, but everything must be strictly verbal, in chain from my superiors to Sasha. Am I understood?"

"You are," Gennadi replied, appalled that the General might have had to risk his own cover to deliver whatever information he brought. "What has happened?"

He couldn't help his mouth falling open as Zinoviy began to talk.

CHAPTER 2

Alois Voss felt the scowl envelope his entire face. Almost painfully so. Across the table, Herr Gerstenberger recoiled a bit, though no words passed between them.

"It is a suicide mission," Alois growled at the man when he finished.

Gerstenberger's hands came up placatingly, like he was trying to calm an angry wolf.

The angry wolf. Wolf-1, commander of the Werewolf Legion.

This man wasn't one of Alois's pilots. Merely the scientific genius that had consulted with men like von Braun and others at places like Peenemünde, where the great rockets and missiles had been designed and tested during the war.

Before the Russians had come. The smarter ones had fled to Austria or the western zones, the former escaping to places like Spain and the latter merely being hauled to America to continue their work.

Better, he supposed, than hanging at the end of a noose. Nuremberg was a name that would live in infamy. A vengeance Alois would see paid in full.

They were operating out of a new air base in Paraguay. Not far from their old one in Argentina, but across national boundaries good enough to keep him from getting arrested. Not safe, but nobody was in this era or this continent.

"I believe that we can make it less of a deathtrap, commander," Gerstenberger offered. "Survivable, even. Care must be taken. Plans developed. Adaptations to the original intent, after all, as so much was lost."

Alois's scowl deepened, but relented some. The man was a genius. Had previously designed for them the great flying wing that Alois would have used to bomb New York City. An Amerikabomber, as Hitler and Goering had envisioned it nearly a decade ago.

Those damnable Russians of the Red Branch had proven that the wing was not a threat, as he'd been far too slow to escape them. And his Werewolf Legion, limited to only four aircraft after the strafing and bombing run, no match in the air.

So he had demanded something faster.

This was the result.

"Let's run through it again," Alois ground out the words. "And explain how we might survive. You are going the wrong direction, after all."

"Understood, commander," Gerstenberger nodded.

They were alone in the man's new workshop office. A place to design new toys. Blueprint them. Then figure out how to build them or pay someone to have parts built. They had enormous depths of funds from gold that had vanished ahead of the American army in 1945.

The table between them had a surface done in brown, suggesting desert. Mostly flat, though ramped up at one end like a hillside. It was the model train track running from end to end that confused him. Vexed him.

Gerstenberger touched it, and the strange car that seemed to hold a silver dart with stubby wings.

Alois took a deep breath, then went ahead and lit a cigarette to calm his nerves.

"We Germans came up with the idea originally," the scientist began. "Eugen Sänger and Irene Bred. It was a design for a liquid-propellant, rocket-powered, sub-orbital bomber intended to strike America from Europe, so high and so fast that nothing could defend against it."

"Sub-orbital?" Alois clarified.

"The theory was that it could reach an altitude of one hundred and forty kilometers or more, flying more than twenty thousand kilometers per hour at the peak," Gerstenberger continued. "From a launch site in German or the occupied territories, they could strike New York or Washington, then continue, staying high in the atmosphere until they came down somewhere in Japanese-held territory in the Pacific."

Alois had heard that before. It still seemed impossible. Worse, Gerstenberger seemed convinced that it could be done.

"We cannot fly from Germany, east to west," Alois reminded the man. "And Japan is done. Flying north from here, where do we land? Siberia? China?"

"Ah, commander, that is where we differ from the Silver Eagle as they originally envisioned it," the man smiled. "I have no intention of building an antipodal bomber. As you note, there is nowhere to flee to, and the missile is hardly maneuverable by more than a simple vector change of only a few degrees."

"Where does it go?" Alois asked.

"Hudson Bay," Gerstenberger smiled.

Alois followed as the man moved to a different table and pulled out maps. From Paraguay to Washington DC or New

York City, the path led inevitably north. To the pole and Russia beyond.

A death sentence.

"Here," Gerstenberger said, tapping the in northern Canada map. "Southhampton Island and Coats Island, near the Hudson Straight. We will place a ship in the vicinity, with small motorboats aboard. The pilots can aim close, then set the autopilot and parachute to safety somewhere near Coral Harbor, where they will be picked up on the shore and sailed safely away before anyone can track them down. You are far enough from any Canadian military forces, as well."

Alois kept his grumbles to himself. Gerstenberger had had to parachute from the Wing, as had Alois, so the scientist had a better understanding of the randomness and difficulties of such a thing.

"Water landing or land?" he asked.

"I think land would be safer, but we will include inflatable rafts with emergency gear," the man replied. "More complicated, but not that much, given the pilots involved."

"Who do you foresee flying this beast?" he asked, turning back to the map table.

"Probably Wolf-3 and his radarman," Gerstenberger replied. "He seems to be the more agile of your other fliers."

Ekkehardt Fischer. The weasel. Yes, better than Wolf-2, but Sigmar was the brute when Alois needed muscle. Ekke was the shiv. This felt like a job for a sharp knife in the dark.

"I believe I understand so far," Alois said, gesturing for the man to continue.

"The sled is on rails," Gerstenberger returned to the train on the table. "It is fired by its own liquid-fueled rockets to get it up to a tremendous speed, then it hits this ski jump, catapulting the Silver Eagle aircraft skyward. The Eagle's rockets and wingtip mounted ramjets would then carry it fully aloft. As we are not intending to fly to Russia, the fuel requirements are less, as are the speeds and altitude needs, so we can carry a significant tonnage of bombs the necessary distance."

"It is a terror weapon," Alois said. "At that speed, could anything be controlled?"

"I envision glide-bombing," the scientist nodded. "The radarman will control the bombs via remote radio packet guidance. You will need a large target, obviously. One with great symbolic value to the Americans. I doubt that you would have the accuracy to strike the Statue of Liberty at these speeds, but the Wall Street district at the south end of Manhattan should be viable."

"Or the newly finished Pentagon that houses the military command of the United States," Alois mused. "The White House as well, using the former as a bullseye and the Washington Monument's spire as a guiding tower. The physical damage will not be great, but the emotional—the morale—value will be exceptional. And the Fuhrer will be avenged, if only a little."

"I had also considered the possibility more recently of somehow decamping our entire structure to the American West, commander," Gerstenberger continued carefully. "Using an American launching point to strike Moscow, but the ranges truly become antipodal at that point. The technology is not mature. And the pilots would have to land in Siberia, which is a death sentence I did not presume would appeal to your wolves."

"No, you are correct," Alois acknowledged. "The final Amerikabomber project for now, to strike one last blow for the Third Reich. After that, I expect that we will have to work on keeping ourselves alive and fed, in a world where fascism has failed for now and those *verdamnt* Americans might be the only thing saving us from the communists."

Both felt the seriousness of that fall upon their shoulders, a wet chilled cloak.

"Are the Americans our only hope of staving off the Slavs?" Gerstenberger pressed quietly.

"Already, Britain implodes under the failure of Empire," Alois nodded. "The French are not far behind them, nor are the Dutch and others. The Russians tried to starve Berlin and push out the western allies. Instead, that catalyzed them into resisting. The Berliners have switched sides. Everything I have heard suggests that a world split into two parts is coming, just as Churchill suggested."

"His Iron Curtain," Gerstenberger murmured.

"Evil, fighting evil," Alois said. "Worse, we may be called upon to fight the communists by the selfsame Americans I wish to punish. Worst, we may find ourselves on the same side as the Red Branch, as I cannot imagine they wish to see their former friends and superiors conquer the world. I would not, having been purged and driven out like a whipped dog."

"Could we ally with them?" Gerstenberger asked, eyes large and nervous.

"I doubt it," Alois shook his head. "They seem to be cast in the mold of international heroes, while this attack, like the one before it had it succeeded, would have made us the worst enemies of civilization."

"Gangsters?"

"As good a name as any," Alois nodded. "I will use terror on my foes. That they might change later does not impact today."

He shook himself and studied the toys in front of him.

"You got this from the Russian?" Alois asked. "Keldysh?"

Gerstenberger nodded.

"Stalin himself was so intrigued by the idea of the Silver Eagle that he sent his son after Sänger and Bredt in France. They refused, so Keldysh has a new design bureau experimenting. This is a version built from his plans, smuggled out by loyal Germans who will never see freedom again, and are willing to assist the Americans in stopping them. I have friends in both places."

Alois understood that. Half of the teams kidnapped by either side and made to work at gunpoint.

It was that or the noose.

"How soon can we start?" Alois asked.

CHAPTER 3

Sasha—the former Soviet Major Aleksandr Kryvenko—would have liked to have done this from the air, but there were only so many things you could learn from photographs taken at a great distance. Especially when his team lacked the sorts of aerial surveillance platform that modern air forces took for granted. Perhaps he would need to build something, someday.

Thus, he was on the ground. In the darkness. Armed. Leading a small team. It would have been nice to bring a larger force, but he needed Lyuba, seated in her aircraft and ready to launch in thirty seconds. And Yuri aloft in his Camel, the camouflaged Ilyushin Il-28 jet bomber that had the range to stay out of sight of the ground, but able to pick up radio signals and relay them.

Sasha wasn't expecting to need *Banshee* to strafe the facility, as she had the Werewolf Legion base, but that wasn't the same as not preparing for such an eventuality.

Instead, he and Vanya had split into two teams. Sasha had brought Ilya Markov, his radarman who was trained in explosives, and Nikon Ilyin, who had flown with Pavel before.

Nikon had spent time in China during the war, studying

their esoteric fighting arts firsthand. Somewhat out of sorts today, without a pilot, so Sasha had taken to flying training missions with the man, keeping him part of the team until a replacement pilot could be found.

Both sets of skills were useful.

Nearby, Vanya—the former Commissar Ivan Zhidkov—had Arkadi Nenashev and his sniper rifle, ready to intervene if necessary. Or rescue them if something went wrong.

They had portable radios. Guns. Dark clothing that still displayed the logo of the Red Branch, because they had managed to be hired by friends of General *Don* Alejandro Navarro y Garcia for this mission. The truck was parked a few kilometers away, hidden in the brush where it would not be found casually.

The compound ahead of them held the enemy. At least so Sasha had been led to believe. Escaped Nazis. Not necessarily mere former German soldiers seeking a new life in Argentina. Those were largely victims of the war, and had already paid a hefty price in being forced to emigrate.

No, he was after the important ones. Those disciples of Mengele or Dornberger who hadn't been taken by the Red Army or the Americans. The ones that had escaped all punishment in fleeing to South America.

Those would be brought to justice, however rough it might end up being. That was why the Red Branch had been created, however secretly that truth might be hidden from the world.

Peron didn't appreciate the pressure of the Americans, demanding that he take sides, so he had invited anyone to come to Argentina. The Pope had created his ratlines to get some of the worst scum out of Europe, but that one was a fascist sympathizer at best, and more likely an active participant.

Millions of dead would never see justice, unless Sasha delivered some measure for them.

He looked at the night sky and nodded. Clear and warm, though cooling as fall began to take hold. Moscow would be in spring, but he doubted that to be an image he could enjoy for years.

But he had accepted his role as Vengeance Personified, however much it also meant exile.

"Two, this is One," he said into the radio. "We're ready."

American kit. Portable. Sufficient range for this, and able to connect to Five overhead.

"One, go ahead," Vanya replied. "We're standing by. No change in target."

Sasha nodded and slipped the device into Ilya's demolition bag for now. The man had a Thompson submachine gun, that American weapon that helped disguise the Soviet origins of Sasha's team. But then, the Americans had armed the world to stop fascism, and all of his people were familiar with US gear.

Sasha drew his Shanxi Type 17 pistol, an oversized copy of the old Mauser C96 broomhandle, redesigned in matching .45 caliber by Chinese warlord Yan Xishan during their Civil War, now almost won by Mao. Better stopping power at short range, and Sasha doubted the need to ever take a shot at five hundred meters.

He turned to Nikon and noted that that one had drawn a weapon he called a rochin. Okinawan, apparently. Sixty-some centimeters of dowel rod with a diamond-shaped metal blade the size of Sasha's hand at one end. Able to stab, slash, or merely stun someone as circumstances demanded.

Sasha had seen the man do slow dance forms with it. Like sword fighting, but not the gentlemanly dueling the French or Germans did on a long rug. Brutal and deadly. Back alley stuff.

Just the sort of thing that Sasha might need tonight.

"Nikon, you lead," he said, following the silent ghost out of the dark brush that had concealed them ere now.

The compound had a wall around it. Old. Adobe over stone. Two and a half meters tall. Enclosing perhaps two hectares of buildings and courtyards inside.

More a statement of purpose than a true defense, as it had sheds and outbuildings that came close enough that they could be used to get over the wall, in addition to several small gates around the sides for gardeners and servants to access the grounds.

Nikon led them to one of the huts, added later and rough-sided enough to climb. He went up the wood and peeked over the wall. Sasha had chosen a dark corner, away from where servants and residents lived, near the garage where several trucks and cars were stored, with more parked outside.

"Clear, sir," Nikon whispered.

Ilya handed him up a rope that had been tied to a nearby tree, in case they needed to climb back out this way later, though there were two gates close enough. And he could always steal a truck and drive through those flimsy barriers if he had to.

Nikon tossed it over, then followed. Sasha went up and looked in, but it didn't appear to have changed at all from pictures taken before.

Over and down, he landed next to Nikon, behind the fender of a Ford sedan. The building remained dark where he could see it, with little external compound lighting on this side. Ilya joined them a moment later in a small puff of dust.

Sasha studied the scene, then pointed.

"That door, I think," he ordered.

Nikon rose and slipped along, stick low to his side where it could flash up and block or strike with equal effectiveness. Sasha had seen it happen. He trailed the man to the small door beside the wider garage door, pistol in hand again and ready for trouble. Ilya followed silently.

Nikon leaned into the door and shoved, but it hadn't been locked, an oversight that they might come to regret later.

Inside it was pitch black, broken only by what little light entered via a pair of high windows.

Ilya closed the door after they entered, and Sasha pulled a small flashlight from his belt, shining it around the bay to reveal the big Mercedes with the top down. Not a staff car as the Nazis had done them, but a distant cousin. Tools nearby. Spare tires. Jumpsuits for mechanics.

No people, which was all he cared about.

Sasha nodded, then followed Nikon to the inner door. Past this, a kitchen, according to reports from spies and visitors that had been passed back to Sasha. Then space for storage and entertaining, with servants at the far end of the ground floor and his target upstairs.

As outside, the inner door was unlocked, the residents secure in their compound and reputation. Nasty Germans who would brook no interference from others.

Sasha didn't care. He was on a mission. Several, in fact, but they all met at the same location.

A dead man.

The hallway was only dimly lit. A rug down the center and wood revealed on the sides. Art that was too dark to see more than lighter and darker bits as they passed.

Nikon made no sound. Sasha made little. Only Ilya, and that less than a cat might.

Kitchen on the right as they approached. Light suddenly

appeared, then disappeared a moment later as the sound of a refrigerator door opening and closing became obvious.

Nikon had frozen. Sasha nodded the man forward, himself and Ilya waiting in the hallway.

Nikon vanished into an open archway without a sound. Then a crack, as the wooden handle of a rochin on a hard skull, followed by a body collapsing to the ground.

Sasha flowed quickly into the room, finding an unconscious man in nicer clothes. Too young to be his target, though, when Nikon turned the face up.

"Dead?" Sasha whispered.

"Merely out," Nikon replied. "What are your orders?"

"Tie him up and gag him for now," Sasha decided. "Employee who shouldn't have to face terminal sanctions for his employer."

After all, Sasha walked a thin ledge. At the end of the day, he was an assassin still secretly working for the GRU. The Party itself. Punishing Stalin's foes.

And the enemies of civilization itself, considering where he was tonight.

Innocents should be protected as much as possible.

If possible.

Nikon worked quickly while Ilya watched the hall and Sasha listened to the silence of the building, settling as the evening cool set in.

Then they were up and in the hallway again.

Nikon paused, pointing at the staircase across and up. Sasha nodded, then gestured Ilya to keep watch from here with his machinegun. As planned, so that they could retreat without being cut off if necessary.

Up, Sasha followed the other man to a landing and then the second floor, where he turned and looked both ways.

Narrower up here than on the ground floor. Same hardwood floors with a rug down the middle. Doors both directions, about half of them open. All dark.

Unlike many mansions or palaces, the master of the home was in the center of the back, where he had a view of the deep gardens. Sasha had decided against approaching from that side, because there were lights on back there much of the time. He assumed that his target would pull the curtains to sleep. Or have a mask that blinded him.

Something.

Double doors directly across. Dark underneath. Closed. Presumably not locked, but Nikon could force them quietly. Or Sasha could kick them in.

He was not feeling benevolent tonight. Even after saving a man who might be a cook.

No, not after hearing how Dornberger had dealt with the slaves that had built his launch platforms for the V-2 rockets. Murdered them all when the project was complete, in order to keep his secrets. Same for the Dutch women he had forced into prostitution, murdering them then bringing in more every two weeks during the construction.

Silence, bought with blood. If the General himself was safe in American hands, his overseers hadn't all made it to America. Tonight, Sasha could almost hear the ghosts crying out to him in their rage.

Still, this had to be done in silence, lest he have to fight his way out afterwards. Most of the people in the compound were probably innocent, save his target. Servants and employees ignorant of the man's crimes didn't deserve to suffer his fate, which was why Sasha hadn't chosen to bomb the place instead.

He drew a breath and again looked both ways before

nodding Nikon into motion and preparing to open fire on moment or sound.

The man slipped silently across the hall and tested the handle, nodding over his shoulder. Sasha rose and crossed, following him into an antechamber of some sort as Nikon opened it. A place for servants or guests to wait their master's emergence.

Sasha closed the door and listened, hearing a hard sawing of an overweight man snoring from the next room. Good enough.

Nikon slipped up and looked in, pausing to check both sides before entering. Sasha followed his Shanxi into the chamber.

Bedroom. Lit by a small light on a bedside table. One man asleep with an eyemask. No wife or mistress present, but nobody had been certain if Herr Oberst Achterberg had either.

Richly decorated room, as might befit a retired Luftwaffe Colonel hiding in South America with the looted goods of a dozen countries. Sasha had been instructed to keep watch for certain things by Colonel Nazarenko, but tonight that was not high on his list. The important wealth would either be in the manor house itself, or stored in a bank's safety deposit box somewhere. Possibly Switzerland, since those parasites cared not a fig for good nor evil if there was profit to be made.

Sasha approached the bed, with the fat mountain of a man sawing lustily at his logs. Eyemask or not, Oberst Achterberg matched the pictures Sasha had been given.

The Pimp of Saint-Omer.

Sasha nodded and pulled a silence from his holster, screwing it onto the barrel of the Shanxi. The .45 cartridge could be made subsonic, but he'd brought standard ammunition tonight. The silencer would reduce that explosion to a loud sneeze at any distance.

Good enough. Except that those ghosts calling out for blood demanded their moment.

Sasha pointed the weapon at the sleeping man and approached close enough to kick the bed lightly. Then harder when that failed to wake him.

Achterberg stirred. Shook his head.

"Wake up, Oberst," Sasha called quietly in German. "You have guests tonight."

The man moved muzzily. Had he gone to bed drunk? Or taken something to sleep?

No, merely a deep sleeper.

A hand came up and removed the eyemask, the eyes underneath blinking large as he recognized the barrel in his face.

"Who?" he started to demand.

"Justice."

Sasha shot him twice to be sure. Both times to the chest, where the bed squeaked loudly as the man thrashed a few times, then fell still.

He turned, but Nikon was watching the front door and showed no signs of worry.

Sasha moved up close, but left the silencer in place for now. Perhaps he would need it again before they escaped.

"Let's go," he said simply.

CHAPTER 4

Sasha had prepared folks by taking a day off from flying, letting his team do some basic maintenance. Or simply read. Whatever they did to relax, though he had confined his people to the base itself.

Base staff had all been approved by General Navarro y Garcia, brought along when he'd transferred their contract to Juan-Manual Hernandez, an Argentine industrialist with supposed communist enemies. Sasha suspected that they were more likely indigenous folk who saw Hernandez as a kulak, just another parasite on society.

As he would have, until forced to play the roll of his own worst enemy.

A message had arrived.

The telegram had been short and coded, but the code was a simple one. A date—today—and the word Dublin, letting Sasha know that that the Colonel would be arriving, with something important to communicate.

Thus, the Red Branch standing down, if only for the day. If Gennadi had traveled this far without much warning, even in his new guise as their White Russian/Irish benefactor, it could not bode well. He had not told everyone else why.

The car arrived. Gennadi greeted folks who had wandered out to see, then smiled as those same folks blanched when the occupant became clear to them. Men and women did not come to attention, but Sasha felt the tension in the air rise.

He greeted the man as an old friend. Gathered up Vanya and Lyuba and the four of them retired to his office with coffee. And the door and window closed. The former for privacy and the latter because fall was coming.

He installed Gennadi behind the desk. Vanya stood with his back to the door. Lyuba took a chair. Sasha leaned against the side wall.

It all looked innocent.

Nobody was fooled.

"The Legion has returned," Gennadi said simply.

Sasha nodded.

General Navarro y Garcia had reported that those men had survived the last encounter. Even those aboard the escort aircraft Vanya and Lyuba had shot down, to say nothing of the one that lost its tail section in a dive trying to escape Sasha.

Voss and the others had obviously bailed out of the Flying Wing before Sasha had killed it, parachuting to safety.

It had been his job to stop an attack on the United States. Not to hunt the entire Legion down and exterminate it. Not even Argentine politics got that crude. Generally.

Or, perhaps, in Argentina, your enemy at breakfast might be an ally by lunch, then fighting a duel to the death with you after dinner.

Sasha really didn't understand how the country worked. If you could call it that.

Many didn't bother trying.

"They have established a new operating base in Paraguay," Gennadi continued. "And a factory building something that appears to be some sort of advanced super rocket, as far beyond the German *Aggregat-4*, known to the west as the V-2, as the A4 was past Chinese fireworks."

"Another Amerikabomber?" Vanya asked simply.

After all, the three of them had stopped the Legion once, attempting such a thing.

"The reports are uncertain," Gennadi acknowledged. "There have been glide tests, static tests, and experimental rocket launches that I am told are extremely scaled down by experts brought in from elsewhere to review the intelligence. There have been enough successes that certain people grow concerned."

"Should someone tell the Americans, instead?" Lyuba asked impishly. "If the Legion is intent on striking them, perhaps they need to invade and do something about it?"

"Berlin has them distracted," Gennadi replied. "They appear to be on the verge of winning, and building Churchill's Iron Curtain into a stone wall athwart the continent. In the east, Mao's Communists have come close to pushing Chiang Kai-shek's Nationalist out of the mainland entirely, where the man has moved much of his force and resources to the island of Formosa. In Washington, a new North Atlantic Treaty Organization will shortly come into being, as it appears that everyone has finally agreed. I do not think that an impending terrorist attack originating in South American will get their attention. Not until it is too late, anyway."

Sasha nodded. The end of the war, almost exactly four years ago, had been a major turning point in human history.

The spring of 1949 felt like another one.

How bad would it get? At least he had gotten his people

safely into the West, where they could operate with some level of autonomy, but was another World War imminent? What would that mean to the Red Branch?

"Sasha?" Gennadi looked up at him, drawing the other two as well.

"How much time do we have?" he asked.

"Not much, given the delays in my learning what was going on," Gennadi replied. "On top of everything else, the information had to climb to the very top levels before it was distributed down to where it crossed my plate."

"Certain individuals not certain they wanted the Legion stopped?" Sasha asked, watching with Vanya and Lyuba stir uncomfortably "Might prefer such a strike that badly demoralized the Americans?"

"Fools who did not listen to history," Vanya growled from the door. "What did such things do to the Londoners? Or Leningrad? Did America surrender after Pearl Harbor? Fools."

"I agree, Vanya," Gennadi replied. "But we are not necessarily party to the decision-makers exercising their will. And the failure in Berlin has angered some and challenged many long-held beliefs in Moscow. Many feel that America needs to be struck now, before it fully re-engages with the world. Their Monroe Doctrine still holds much value, even as Truman appears to be set to overcome it with men like Acheson and Kennan."

"And such a thing as this would ignite in them a fury unseen in modern history, Gennadi," Sasha snapped, barely stopping short of calling him *Colonel*. "They will be terrible in their vengeance."

"How many people in positions of power are convinced that they can divert the Americans into punishing South America?" Lyuba asked coldly, a glass of water thrown metaphorically in his face that stopped Sasha instantly. "Whittling away their power? Frittering it away mindlessly, even as China comes to some sort of terrible conclusion? Does this cause them to turn their back on Berlin at the most critical moment, allowing Stalin to take all of Europe in his hand?"

Sasha could see it. The man he had been, before, would have even welcomed such an outcome, he suspected, but Major Kryvenko had been a patriot. A *New Soviet Man*, intent on remaking the world into a place without empires and colonies. Without need or fear, as Roosevelt himself had once demanded of humanity.

Before Comrade Colonel Nazarenko had challenged *Sasha* to save the world. All of them, really, but the Red Branch was his mission. His legacy.

"What kind of defenses does the Werewolf Legion retain?" Sasha asked, putting aside all thought of the arcs of empires now to step up and stop evil. "We were merciless in destroying them before."

"They have acquired many older aircraft," Gennadi replied, turning to face him. "Nothing that can dance with the Nightviper, but the Paraguayan air forces nearby are both better run and more paranoid than the Argentine, especially after the civil war and coup attempts over the last several years. I doubt that three Nightvipers could succeed against an angry air group. Or even a wing. This is a mission on the ground. You will have to sneak in and see what can be done, because I have aerial photographic evidence that their base is probably as well defended against bombing as the Kremlin itself. Dozens of guns of various sizes."

"Do they know we are coming?" Vanya asked crisply.

"They are prepared for someone," Gennadi said with a shrug. "If not the Red Branch, perhaps the American Marine

Corps. Someone. *Banshee* greatly spooked them with her singular attack, because those men had apparently forgotten the Night Witches."

Sasha grinned. The famous and deadly 46th Taman Guards Night Bomber Aviation Regiment, who flew canvas and wood biplanes, at night, to bomb and strafe German positions. Often while turning off their propellers to come in as silent as a witch on a broom.

Perhaps not all that effective as a military solution, but the psychological damage they had inflicted on the Nazis had been immense.

And Lyuba had been one of the best of them to survive.

"So we must reconstitute ourselves as a commando?" Sasha asked.

"That is correct," Gennadi replied. "When we built this force, you and I, we understood that some missions could only be done on the ground. Thus, I provided you with a wealth of skills and experience that went far beyond merely the best pilots I could find. I gave you the Red Branch. You must now use it."

Sasha nodded, sobered.

Achterberg had been destroyed. Vengeance served. And there were others, but they would have to wait.

How did he prevent World War Three?

CHAPTER 5

Alois drove the Jeep out to where the Eagle was landing, leaving the rest of his wolves back at the hangar or following on in a slower truck that could tow it back.

He had flown the mock-up previously. Felt the power of the smaller rocket engines ignite as he separated from the tow plane and tested the aerodynamics of the thing. Not as big as this one, the one that would bomb the United States, but close enough for his purposes.

It came to rest at the end of the runway, a long dart, flat on top and bottom, with stubby, rectangular wings both towards the front as canards as well as the rear. Extremely low aspect ratio on the double, tandem wings. One vertical stabilizer that also extended below the fuselage about twenty centimeters. A cockpit with two seats, front and back. Needle-tipped prow for cutting through the thin air. Bicycle landing gear with secondary wheels that deployed below the wingtips, mostly to hold it upright on the ground during testing, though they would be removed before the final flight.

This craft would not need to land after that.

The canopy had retracted by the time he got there. The

thing was on short landing gear, so Ekke—Ekkehardt Fischer, Wolf-3—was able to climb out without a ladder, followed by his navigator/radarman, Lars Weber.

The two men wore pressurized suits with dark helmets that would hold air and heat, nobody entirely certain what things would be like above fifty thousand meters, other than it would be cold and empty. Not orbital space, but higher than perhaps anyone had ever flown. The land of Verne, perhaps.

The dark helmets came off now as he parked the Jeep and got out.

"How does it fly?" Alois asked.

"Badly at slow speeds," Ekke confirmed, echoing Alois's earlier assessment. "But that is the lack of wing surface and the limited movement of the controls. If this were intended for more than a single mission, we might consider secondary controls with greater play."

"And the ramjets?" Alois asked.

That had been today's test. The sled would accelerate the Eagle to faster than the speed of sound, at which point it would detach and lift off. The Eagle itself had several small rocket motors that would provide thrust, but each of the forward canards had a special ramjet installed. The tow plane had lifted the Eagle aloft, then gotten it up to an altitude where Ekke could dive, providing enough forward speed for the ramjets to function properly.

It had left a streak of gray smoke across the sky.

"You aim at a hole in the sky and blast through it, commander," Ekke said simply. "I believe Doctor Gerstenberger when he suggests that we will be at five times gravity while all three systems are operating. Here, it drove us both into our seats for twenty seconds, but I was still able to operate. The autopilot will handle the hardest parts of acceleration. Of that, I am certain."

Alois agreed. He'd drawn about two Gs with just the mockup's rockets burning. Combining all three would produce an incredible amount of thrust, even if just for a short time.

Idly, he'd wondered if such a design could be used to create a proper spaceplane, as people were starting to call it. Launch from the ground with enough power and fuel to get up to an orbital insertion.

Gerstenberger claimed that metallurgical technology would need to create far lighter and stronger alloys first, while also finding more efficient fuels to burn, because he had calculated that at least ninety-eight percent of take-off weight of a normal rocket would be made up of just those two things, leaving pitifully little for a man and all the other tools necessary to keep him alive and bring him home.

Worse, as he had started his work, Gerstenberger had gone back to the original calculations by Sänger and Bredt and found a previously-unknown error, showing that the heat flow during the initial atmospheric re-entry would have been greater than the original they had calculated. Their craft would have melted instead of gliding and bouncing across the thin air at altitude.

Fixable entirely, but that would necessitate more weight for improving the thing the Doctor called a heat shield, thus increasing the base mass yet more, in an ongoing and perhaps infinite recursion loop of design and engineering.

Luckily, they were not intending to go as fast. Or as high. Or as far.

Still, he intended to send along a pair of bombs to attack the Pentagon, Truman apparently staying in a nearby building while the White House itself was being renovated. Not that destroying the building itself would be a bad thing symbolically, but to travel that far and not have a chance at Truman as well simply meant that the pentagram on the river would be the goal instead.

Alois saw the two men into his Jeep as Sigmar arrived in the truck and ground crew began the process of getting the Eagle ready for the next flight.

He drove them back to the hangar, ignoring the men outside the fence, lined up to watch the strange aircraft that they could see, but not approach. Nobody was allowed inside the wire who was not Werewolf Legion. Even supplies were delivered to a nearby warehouse outside, then carefully packed over by men Alois had selected. The Paraguayan Air Force stayed over there.

He had managed to turn one of the Russian pilots in the Red Branch, an inveterate black marketeer whose corruption had been exacerbated by the West, though Kryvenko had killed the man before their first final confrontation.

Alois turned his head to the various airmen watching.

Too many people knew about this mission. Knew about the spaceplane.

Worse, he could not eliminate all of them later to keep his secrets, so it would likely be necessary to flee from South America entirely after this.

Did he offer his services to the French or British next? The Americans would be overwhelmingly angered, he knew, but Alois intended to plant stories blaming the Communists for the attack anyway.

Merely reading the newspapers each day made it clear that the wartime alliance of convenience to stop Germany had unraveled entirely. And many of his old friends and cohorts had ended up captured by the Americans. He could see their fingerprints on changes in American behavior, though truth be told, the Americans had always acted like imperialists in the world.

They had finally decided to confront the communists fully. To return to the Civil War backing the Whites.

It was a pity that they could not be allies. But the French tended to hate everyone, so if he portrayed himself as a devout anti-communist freedom fighter, they might hire him. They and the British were having troubles as their various overseas empires began to melt under Stalin's relentless pressure. Mao would only make it worse in the East as he consolidated his hold on China.

"You are quiet, commander," Ekke observed as they got under cover and he parked the Jeep.

"Weber, you get cleaned up," Alois told the third man. "I wish to debrief Wolf-3 first, then both of you in a while."

All of them exited the vehicle, Alois leading Ekke into his office and closing the door.

He poured some schnapps and lit a cigarette. Ekke did the same.

"Trouble, sir?" Wolf-3 asked as they sat, facing each other across the desk.

"The world has changed, even since we escaped Argentina and began this mission, Fischer," Alois replied. "The Third Way that Peron preaches might have already begun to fail, leaving us trapped in a binary choice."

"Sir?"

"The Americans are pushing back on the Russians," Alois said. "Hard. And I fully intend to strike them at least once for all that they did to us and the Reich. It is the morning after that that concerns me."

"Should we move everything to Africa, sir?" Ekke countered. "Bomb the Kremlin instead? Or someplace in Iraq? The British have ended the occupation, though they still control everything. Could we launch from there, cross the pole, and still land in Canadian waters?"

It was a compelling idea. Strike the communists a hard blow at the moment when they looked close to triumphing in Europe. Perhaps kill Stalin, if they could destroy the Kremlin.

But he owed the Americans. They had been the ones to defeat Hitler, for all of Stalin's claims that the Soviet Union had won the war. They had merely provided a wall of dead bodies for the German army to stumble on. To choke on.

The Americans had armed them with endless supplies of equipment and thrown them at the Wehrmacht.

"I will speak with Gerstenberger," Alois temporized. "There would need to be whole new sets of calculations to run, and that takes time to do by hand. Perhaps we can make a second missile and a second mission later."

Ekke nodded and sipped, watching him.

"I am concerned about the tomorrow that rises after the Pentagon is in flames," Alois continued. Alone with Sigmar—Wolf-2—he could discuss these things, the four of them with Gerstenberger being the core of the Legion in many ways. "We will need to be entirely packed up and ready to leave the instant your Silver Eagle takes to the air, Ekke. And I will need to determine where we can flee to. Where we can find work, while the Americans get over their anger at what you will do to them."

"Will they?" he asked.

"They hired men like von Braum and Dornberger without hesitation," Alois laughed cruelly. "They want power more than purity of their so-called American Way. If we let it be known that the Soviets have been secretly funding us and hired the Legion to do the thing, perhaps with some extravagant blackmail suggestions thrown in, I think we can distract them. Or perhaps go work for the French, as they have little respect for a new American order that treats them as an after-thought much of the time."

"I will fly the Eagle," Ekke shrugged. "You will tell me where. And who to kill. And where to go when the ship picks us up in Canada."

And he would. All of the Legion were fanatically devoted Nazis. It was simply that his values more and more appeared to align with the very men who had been his enemies four years ago.

Not his worst enemies. Those lived in Moscow, Leningrad, and Stalingrad. Even the purged Russians of the Red Branch— Kryvenko and his lot—were merely mercenaries who had been hired by that Argentinian fop to stop him from using the Flying Wing to destroy the Statue of Liberty.

No, it was entirely possible that he would have to find a way to placate the Americans into hiring him somehow, after getting his revenge on them.

A delicate wire to walk, but he had sworn an oath to his Fuhrer.

He would see it done.

CHAPTER 6

Lyuba had chosen to fly today, while others packed things. She always traveled light, an outgrowth of the Witches need to be light at all times, so packing wouldn't take her long. Instead, she had taken Yanina Chumak into the air, keeping their skills sharp as they flew mock-strafing runs on hills outside of town.

The Nightviper could even haul bombs, but had none at the present. Still, practice. Fast, low, and deadly. Pretending that there were more Nazi tank units below them that needed to be bombed in silence.

There was no silence today.

As she pulled back from another run, chasing sky, Yanina spoke.

"You are tense," her partner and radar-operator noted quietly, using the inside intercom system because not every conversation needed to be broadcast.

Lyuba glanced over, and immediately skipped trying to convince the woman otherwise. In addition to everything else, Yanina was the team's Flight Nurse, so she watched. And knew.

"We are not taking the vipers to Paraguay," Lyuba offered.

"Possibly not taking the Camel, though that can be a useful cargo carrier for priority things that need to be quickly delivered."

"You are concerned that Sasha will not have a role for you in what comes?" Yanina pressed.

Outside, the clouds had gotten thick and low. No rain, but a threat impending.

The Nightviper around her would not care. It was an all-weather fighter. Not restricted to daylight operations, because it had radar. And an exceptional operator. Both of them.

"Worse," Lyuba admitted, finding the words even as her hands automatically brought the nose around and began the planning for another run.

Bombing this time. Low and fast, as if using light bombs to take out a small building with surprise.

It required touch, as you had little time to maneuver, so the instant the bombs were clear of the rack, you had to stand on one ear and blast clear, without losing altitude or speed.

"Worse?"

"You are our nurse," Lyuba continued. "If we break into teams, do you and I get automatically held back out of danger as a support element? Sasha might not intend it that way, but is he protecting us from danger unconsciously because of our gender?"

Silence from her partner and friend let Lyuba know she had struck a telling blow. Yanina was not a warrior, though she had bombed the Germans from rear seat of a Polikarpov. She was a nurse now, her career after being demobilized, though it put her in the perfect spot to join the Red Branch.

"You might not be wrong," Yanina offered. "Have you spoken with him?"

"I have not." Lyuba admitted to her cowardice finally. "I have been there when he needed me, doing the jobs the Red Branch required of us. Paraguay vexes me."

She felt Yanina's nod, so close they were physically as well as emotionally.

"Pavel was a black marketeer, before it proved to be the death of him," Yanina finally said, as Red-3 began a howling dive intended to frighten a flock of sheep that were troops and a truck in her mind.

Targets.

"And we have a sniper in Arkadi," Lyuba replied as she executed the run perfectly. "An explosives expert in Ilya. Close combat in Nikon. Nurse. Mechanical genius. Actor. What role remains open for *Banshee*, when the team is grounded?"

"You are also an aeronautical engineer and designer," Yanina pointed out. "One capable of creating better systems, better aircraft, for the Red Branch."

"All the more reason that Sasha might hold me back," Lyuba countered. "Such folks do not *fight*."

A pause. Longer. Yanina had never been an officer. Not the woman's mindset. A follower, of sorts. Or rather, an incredibly strong-willed woman, highly intelligent, but willing to subsume herself into a role as part of a team.

Exactly as Lyuba did, but Yanina didn't chafe at the confines.

"I hesitate," Yanina said as Lyuba decided that she had frightened the animals enough for one day and turned the Nightviper's nose home.

"Yes?" Lyuba asked.

"Is it demeaning to suggest that your Ukrainian beauty could be used as a weapon?" Yanina finally said.

Lyuba kept her sour scowl inside. She had considered such a thing. Wondered if the Colonel had looked at several Night Witches he might recruit, and filtered them for the prettiest one. It was an unbecoming comment, even in her mind, but it still bit.

And it was something that none of the men could do, as demeaning as it might be.

Whatever the team needed? Whatever Sasha needed?

Lyuba suppressed the growl.

"And perhaps you should put your dancer's legs and body to work as an acrobat?" Yanina asked.

Lyuba glanced over at the woman's smile. Yanina had dark hair. Slavic bones. Built thick like Russian peasant, but with a lovely singing voice.

"Acrobat?" Lyuba asked, anger giving way to intrigue.

"Climb. Jump. Shoot," Yanina nodded. "Flair out to one side like a proper wing and catch an enemy in a flank unseen. Unexpected. As you did when Pavel proved to be a criminal after all?"

Lyuba owned that. She had shot Pavel in the back, when he had been about to kill Sasha. Not many people knew she had fired the round. Her. Yanina. Sasha.

As the runway at the base came into view, she nodded, watching pieces fall into place.

"Yes," she said. "Vanya will hold with a sniper, and perhaps a nurse. Sasha will lead with Ilya and Nikon. I can drift off from that group as needed and do things with surprise, because how many men will never even notice that I have a face?"

Yanina laughed. It was a cruel, mocking sound.

"Many of our own men never see mine," Yanina said, knowing that Lyuba only had eyes for Sasha anyway. Yanina found herself surrounded by many men, all of whom pursued her, though she had made it clear that settling down and raising a family was for someone else.

Too many adventures ahead.

Lyuba understood that in her bones.

CHAPTER 7

The flight to Paraguay was nearing its end.

Sasha still remembered that stolen an old Martin B-10 bomber that had been converted to a civilian airliner. Taken as part of his escape from the Werewolf Legion. A revolution at the time of its construction though that time had been 1934. Utterly archaic today.

Plus, it had belonged to the Legion, so he had simply abandoned it on a runway after landing, where someone had later come and quietly flown it home, nobody mentioning the terrible dogfights that had taken place nearby.

Mercenaries didn't get emotional. That was in the job description. They got hired to do a job, did it, and went on to the next contract. If the Red Branch had inflicted a cruel and humiliating blow on the Werewolf Legion, everyone woke up the next morning and ignored it.

Sasha didn't believe that for a moment, but also didn't let it bother him. He had bigger problems to address.

Today, Señor Hernandez had arranged for a DC-3 to carry them into Paraguay, ostensibly as a vacation for his flying teams, leaving Yuri and Dmitri behind to supervise the base, though Sasha did take Oleg the actor with him.

They would be staying in Asuncion, just across the river from Argentina and down-country from the spots still argued over with Bolivia from time to time.

The Werewolves had taken over part of an air base north of town. Not far, but there were no other bases where the Red Branch might operate, even if he had wanted to bring his Nightvipers with him.

Paraguay was even less stable than Peron's Argentina these days, having just emerged from yet another low-level civil war that had been lost to the government's forces. Still chaotic, but not as stirred up as Argentina, but that was Peron himself inviting anyone and everyone who wanted to come.

Including those needing to escape whatever crimes they might have committed elsewhere. Sasha could not punish them all, but that wasn't going to stop him trying.

From the sky, Asuncion was a pretty town filling the eastern bank of the long river as it slowly expanded to the entire valley floor. North and east, the terrain turned heavier. Mountainous, or at least hills that would conceal things from the air. Or any distance.

He had maps. Photographs that Gennadi had delivered, along with what tidbits the spies had been able to tease out.

Nobody could help him, though. The Red Branch was an independent mercenary company, operating without flags though all of his people were ex-Soviet. Mostly Ukrainian, but the Russians had always relied on their southern neighbors to be tougher than those pretty boys from the northwest, or the Mongols from the east.

Vanya had been reading a file. He closed it now and started

to slide it home in a leather satchel that normally carried his flight maps before stopping himself.

"Sasha, we do not have much time," Vanya announced.

"Oh?" Sasha asked, watching him across the central aisle.

Sasha had a row to himself, with Ilya keeping Nikon company a row back. Otherwise, people tended to sit in team pairs.

"Looking at what Gennadi proposes, I think that they have now tested all of the component parts of the aircraft successfully," Vanya nodded. "Lyuba, could you look at page ten and eleven and let me know your thoughts?"

He handed it forward a row to the woman, then they waited as she digested.

Aeronautical engineer. Also a test pilot, but even the Soviet authorities occasionally forgot that women were just as capable as men. And the 46th even moreso. Especially *Banshee*.

She read quickly as he watched her ear and jaw. Utterly gorgeous. Brilliant.

If they were not pilots together...

He crushed that thought as she turned, knees coming out into the aisle so she could see them.

"I agree," Lyuba announced simply. "They have tested the rocket engines in a mock-up. Glide-tested the smaller aircraft as well as the larger one. Ramjet tests appear successful, but a ramjet is a simple-enough tool to use, once you understand it. The sled has undergone various tests, both for acceleration and actually casting a dead weight glider mock-up into the air. There does not appear to be many more tests necessary before they are ready to launch their attack."

She hesitated there, brow furrowed, then moved to the rear of the file, flipping back and forth until she found the page she was looking for.

"And, they have begun packing again," she said, marking a paragraph and handing it to Sasha.

He read quickly, seeing the same thing she did.

After losing all of their experimental Blackhawk aircraft to *Banshee*'s strafing and then in aerial combat, they had returned to flying old Warhawks and other American propeller aircraft. Nothing that could fight a Nightviper, save in massed numbers, much as Vanya had talked about the early days of his war, losing horrible percentages of his squadrons to kill only a few Nazi pilots, knowing that the Germans were better trained and equipped at the time.

A war won on blood and patience, rather than elegant skill. That had come later, once the Americans had provided vast air armadas that people like Sasha and Yuri had helped ferry in from places like Persia.

Sasha nodded to Vanya.

"As she noticed, they pack," Sasha acknowledged the woman's insight. "The aircraft are not theirs, so those will be left behind or sold. Personnel are getting ready to depart, though we cannot tell where they will flee to."

"Would they stay in Paraguay?" Vanya asked.

"They likely would not even remain in South America," Lyuba countered. "This will anger the Americans terribly, as you note. They will lash out in their fury. Best to vanish for a time. Especially if you do not need to bring aircraft with you, save perhaps in crates for later. Get to a port and catch a ship somewhere."

Sasha wondered where Voss might go, but that was not today's concern. Today, he had to somehow stop the man from launching another attack. One that might possibly ignite the very World War everyone grew concerned was imminent.

Imperial colonialism was dying. Slowly. Painfully. Unwillingly. Irreversibly nonetheless.

Communism had begun to infect people. If it was too much the nationalism of Stalin rather than the universal globalism of Trotsky, it was still clawing at the toes of the old imperial order in places where the wealthy held everything and the poor were nothing but modern-day serfs.

The Americans and their banker overlords would never allow revolution. Would fight war after war to keep those bankers in power, one leather jackboot on the throats of the poor who merely wanted to be free. To live free.

A new world was fighting to be born, and Gennadi had chosen him to help, in his own way, by killing and destroying those elements of the old regime that would not gracefully retire from the world stage to let socialism progress on the way to true communism as Marx and Engels had foreseen.

Old Nazis for now. Perhaps old kulaks later.

First, he had to stop the fools who were playing with fire in a room filled with gunpowder, threatening to blow up the world.

If he could.

Sasha turned and located Corporal Oleg Markov. Ilya's younger brother and a man who spoke at least a dozen languages fluently, for reasons he had never been willing to share. He waved the man close, even as the aircraft began its descent into Asuncion.

"Sir?" Oleg asked.

"As soon as we land, you disappear," Sasha ordered. "Take whoever you need with you and find out how one might best get to any coast from here, carrying cargo requiring flatbed rail cars or five-ton trucks. We don't know how the Legion will flee or where, but *Banshee* is correct, and we must be able to tell Gennadi where to look. Questions?"

Oleg paused. Looked inward. Turned his head.

"Nikon, I'll need you," he called simply.

Sasha nodded and handed the file back to Vanya.

They could strike quickly, if needed. Not strafe and bomb, given the defenses Voss had erected around himself this time, but get in on the ground and do things. He would take the rest of the team to see, but *packing* instead of packed suggested that they still had a few days.

If he was lucky.

Because even a Nightviper could not stop a Silver Eagle once it was aloft.

PART TWO

ASUNCION

CHAPTER 8

Oleg owed the Major his life.

At the critical moment, when every avenue of possible escape had closed off, leaving only a gulag somewhere in Siberia, Major Kryvenko had needed the Red Branch. Oh, certainly it had been Colonel Nazarenko that had come to take him out of that cell, but that man had merely understood that Stárshiy Leytenánt Yuri Datsyuk had needed a radio man for the Camel. And it wasn't Dmitri Yefimov, distant cousin to the great flying hero.

Dmitri could fix anything. He didn't talk to people.

Brother Ilya had already belonged. Had put in a good word for his little *брат*, who liked to make funny faces, tell silly stories, impersonate other bodies, and make people laugh.

Commissars rarely had a sense of humor. Especially with an actor who can vanish inside a role and occasionally forgets to turn it off again later.

He was safe with the Red Branch. Able to study languages, listening to every radio station and channel he could find on the longwave, understanding a remarkable many of them with the help of the BBC World Service.

If he didn't especially look dark enough to be a native of Paraguay, neither did a great many other people on the streets as he and Nikon walked.

Nikon spoke Spanish like an immigrant. Rough. Slow. Balky. At the same time, his English was also getting better, so Oleg could introduce him as a friend from London.

Oleg could pass for a native, having been here long enough to sound it.

And if he didn't do the sorts of stupid black market dealings that Red-4 had done before it got Pavel Zaslavsky killed, Oleg knew how to talk to people. How to find them. Find things. Negotiate deals. An actor inside his roles.

They were down on the riverfront. He would start here, because shipping things to Buenos Aires would be easiest on a barge. Trains would be harder, but possible, and that opened up distant places like Sao Paulo in Brazil or Porto Alegre in Uruguay.

Still, everything would have to be transported from that base to Asuncion before it could go anywhere.

They walked in civilian attire. Suits of a British cut, seen by anyone with any fashion knowledge. Good enough to mark them as outsiders for now, which was his intent.

Oleg did not know what gangs might run these docks, and wished to not be seen immediately as a threat to their control.

His friends were far from here and the locals might play rough.

He found a bar that looked appropriate. Populated by the right people, being less workers and more middle managers, if he could make a clean distinction. Still on the rough side of things, so hopefully a bit underground.

Wine instead of beer, again leaning in towards a higher

class of ruffian that might be interested in talking. Eyes watched them enter, but lips remained pursed.

As expected. They drank and watched. Were watched. Nikon spoke in English, loud enough to be heard as such, though he could probably follow the quiet whispers around the room.

Oleg certainly did.

Folks came and went. Frequently talked to an older man in the corner. Gnarled hands showing a lifetime of work. White hair. Bright eyes. Good suit.

Oleg made eye contact with the man to get his attention. Waited. Others came and went and he was largely ignored.

"Now what?" Nikon asked.

"Now, we wander off and hope that someone is interested enough to ask us questions," Oleg said, rising.

Nikon was confused, but that was fine. He was along for his deadly hands, rather than his mind.

They exited, then crossed the street. Oleg found a kiosk on the corner and bought a newspaper and a chocolate bar, both better than anything he could have gotten back home, even in Leningrad.

Poverty had been a necessity to withstand evil. He had fought for five years, since he'd been sixteen, to stop the Nazis, somehow surviving when so many others had fallen.

Now, they had money. Access to all the debaucheries of the West, because they were mercenaries. Rich, by many standards. He would not allow it to flavor his views. Pavel Zaslavsky had gotten himself killed because he could not transcend the American concept of a child in a candy store with a dime.

Instead, Oleg found a telephone pole and leaned against it, apparently reading his paper while Nikon kept watch over his shoulder.

"A man comes," Nikon murmured.

Oleg watched the rest of the street. Nobody was watching them with any more emphasis than neighborhood gossips and old women. *Babushkas* were the same the world over. He had little to hide from them, because they would see the role and not the purpose.

"Trade me sides," Oleg muttered, turning to watch the older man from the bar cross the street warily, himself buying the afternoon news as well and stepping nearby as though reading it.

"Strange times," the man offered blandly in English, perhaps two meters away if someone was watching.

Not close enough to be a meeting. Not far enough away to be ignored.

"Strangers in town," Oleg countered equally, a bit more quiet, though the street was noisy with vehicle traffic. "Noting the terrain and hoping we might find someone who could provide information for a price not too steep."

He left it at that, turning the page as though ignoring everything.

The man had sidled perhaps a half-step closer in turning his own paper. Oleg was impressed with the man as an actor, too.

"What information?" the man asked quietly.

"Other strangers," Oleg replied. "Doing certain things upcountry, but preparing to perhaps pack up everything and leave, possibly in the dead of night. Possibly tomorrow, even."

"Upcountry?" The man was intrigued. "Things sent out of country pass through Asuncion."

"Thus, our arrival," Oleg replied, nodding vaguely. "And seeking experts on various topics."

"Are you staying long?"

As in, is this a relationship? Or merely two ships passing like a prostitute and her john?

"I am merely a messenger," Oleg replied. "My commander is staying nearby tonight and hoped that we might find him information."

"Oh?"

Oleg gave him the name of the hotel and the name *Cernunnos*. Kryvenko might draw flies. Red Branch might draw secret police and Paraguayan or Argentine spies, but the Celtic reference codename under which Major Kryvenko flew should be adequate.

"He would greatly appreciate if someone with local expertise might be prepared to trade money for discretion," Oleg continued.

"I shall make inquiries," the stranger offered, then folded up his newspaper and tucked it under one arm before departing.

"What just happened?" Nikon asked after a moment.

"We have made contract with what might be the local underworld," Oleg replied. "Possibly the secret police, but I cannot imagine them to be that sophisticated around here. They lack commissars like Vanya Zhidkov to do it correctly. No, those types are usually too flamboyant in their corruption to succeed, relying instead on the bribes they take to survive, until someone burns them."

"Spoken from experience?" Nikon asked.

Oleg shrugged. He had done what he had to survive during the war. Afterwards, it had just meant fewer people actually shooting at him.

Not less risk.

He did keep watch, though, he led Nikon the other direction. Who knew which of those *babushkas* drew a secondary income selling tall tales to secret policemen who might sit in fancy bars and never actually get into the sewers looking for trouble?

The Major would need to be prepared.

Oleg owed that man everything.

CHAPTER 9

Vanya had learned to keep his mouth shut about the things that happened around him. Gennadi had asked him to provide a moral backbone to the Red Branch, but that had been utterly unnecessary. Sasha would never bend.

Instead, Vanya's job was frequently to provide a calming influence on the others. Pavel had been the worst, but *Banshee* was a wildcat barely tamed and always in motion.

The enlisted men were the ones that he watched. Sober. Reflective. He would say superior, but Vanya tried to present himself as logical and thoughtful instead of an officer in charge. A professor, if you would, standing to one side of the man with the movie-star good looks and lantern jaw.

Sasha was as formidable as he was impressive.

The visitor looked tiny by comparison, but no less intimidating in his own way. An older man, marked by the darker tones of the native population rather than the Spaniards who often ruled.

Oleg Markov had admitted him to the room, then set Ilya, Nikon, and Arkadi outside to protect the meeting. Lyuba wore her blue jacket with the bib closed. Open, it drew the eye towards her chest instead of her eyes. Even Vanya had to break himself out of being mesmerized occasionally.

The stranger had joined her, him, and Sasha as the fourth point at a table, drinking Irish whiskey because they were an Irish organization. At least as far as anybody outside needed to know. Vanya spoke English and Spanish with just enough accent to be an outsider. Sasha always sounded mid-Atlantic American.

"This rocket," Markov's underworld guest nodded. "There are many rumors about such a thing. Some range into the fantastical, leapfrogging South America into the front row as a world power."

Vanya kept his sourness to himself. Little that he had learned or seen in the last year had brought him any expectation that South America was ever catching up with the European or North American powers. If anything, he could see the world splitting into north and south components soon, even as China joined the Socialist ranks. They would at least rebuild with Stalin's assistance, just as Japan was only down until such time as they could get their feet under them again with American assistance.

Three worlds coming? It was an interesting thought. He would perhaps write himself a letter later to explore such thoughts, before burning it if it contained any elements that might bring trouble to the Red Branch.

They were still spies, at the end of the day. Hired assassins, though nobody spoke much of such things.

"The rocket is unlikely to change the balance of power," Lyuba offered. "It is a singular invention, though it does present interesting technological advances. We presume that it will be fired once, then the men responsible will immediately depart."

The stranger watched her with new eyes, perhaps finally seeing past the beauty to the immense intellect hidden inside. Sometimes hidden.

"And you wish to know where they go?" the man asked, turning to Sasha.

"Already, they appear to be packing up," Sasha replied. "We would like to know how much they are shipping. And where to, because of hints and suggestions that they will leave South America entirely."

"Why would they need to leave?" the man demanded voice wounded. "Unless they were doing something so heinous that..."

He tapered off there. Vanya nodded, along with the other three.

So terrible that someone would unleash devastation in its wake.

And if the perpetrators had fled, how many innocents might be caught up in the explosion, collateral damage to the thing?

"It is a weapon," Sasha replied calmly.

Perhaps as calmly as Vanya might have. Perhaps.

"A weapon?"

"We are the Red Branch," Sasha said, turning his torso sideways and tapping the blue kite shield patch with the red stag whose horns held up a white globe.

The man nodded warily. News had not traveled far out of Argentina, but that was everyone involved quietly pretending that nothing had happened, once Sasha had destroyed the Flying Wing.

"Last winter, we stopped a group attempting to bomb New York City from a base in Argentina," he continued calmly. "The Werewolf Legion. These same men are building a rocket plane. And the flight it will take points slightly west of due north. It cannot be stopped in the air."

"And they launch another attack on the Yankees?" he asked, voice dripping with disdain, but Vanya was not surprised.

In South America, only the wealthy were happy to deal with the American military. The entire point of the US Marine Corps seemed to be overthrowing countries and creating literal banana republics, pliable fools dominated by bankers. Owned by them, in fact.

"On civilization itself," Sasha countered sharply.

From any other man, Vanya knew it would sound arrogant. Sasha could make you believe. The man was a hero.

"You think the Americans would attack Paraguay?" the stranger asked, voice dripping with sarcasm and contempt.

"I think they might send bomber fleets to punish someone for attacking them," Sasha replied, dropping the temperature in the room to the point than Vanya feared frostbite might occur. "Anyone. *Everyone.*"

That got through. Americans angry enough to to do Asuncion what they had done to Berlin. Or Tokyo.

Or Hiroshima.

As long as they had the monopoly on atomic bombs, who knew what arrogance the Americans might stumble into? Especially if provoked.

"How do we stop it?" the man asked, personality almost inverting in a heartbeat as the thoughts of his home being annihilated by nuclear fire become something more than a punchline.

"We will stop them," Sasha replied. "That is what the Red Branch does. Do not speak of it outside this room, though. Afterwards, they will attempt to flee us. To leave you and your country holding the bag, as it were. To be punished for *their* sins. They cannot escape me. They can never escape me. You will tell me where they go, and I will chase them down. I am *Cernunnos* of the Wild Hunt."

The man was white. Drained. Vanya felt almost as bad. *Banshee* had a hard, cold smile on her face, but she was another excitable one like Sasha.

And they had spoken, the three of them, about saving the world, like it might become a job requirement.

The *raison d'être* of the Red Branch itself, if he could say that without sounding like some Cassandra from legend.

Except that it might get that bad.

CHAPTER 10

Sasha looked up at the knock. He and Vanya shared a room in the hotel, largely staying out of sight after they had sent their new underworld contact off to do things for them and Oleg had taken Arkadi into town to arrange transport for the team, because time was short.

Vanya was at the table working, with Sasha seated on his bed, so the Commissar opened the door to Lyuba. He waved her in.

"Problems?" Sasha asked, putting down his papers at the look of stark crossness on the woman's face.

She moved directly to the table, so he and Vanya joined her.

"I have been studying the mathematics necessary to build and successfully fly a Silver Eagle," she announced solemnly.

Sasha nodded. Aeronautical engineer, as well as test pilot. As well as beauty and killer and a vast array of other things.

"Some of the more recent work of folks like Keldysh talk of an antipodal bomber," she continued. "A thing that can make a single, sub-orbital flight to land on the other side of the world from launch."

"What is opposite Paraguay?" Sasha asked.

She paused, looking at some unseen point.

"The western Pacific ocean, just off the coast of China, somewhat south of Formosa, I believe," she replied. "Irrelevant in any case, as only a suicidal fool would want to fly that far in a rocket."

"Where would you try to land, then?" Vanya asked.

"Canada," she nodded. "Keep going north from New York City. Hudson Bay is more or less in a straight line. Ditch somewhere close to water, and have a ship come and pick you up. It provides an easy point of escape, especially as everyone will be looking the wrong way. And New York City burning."

"Two ships?" Sasha asked, seeing the shape of the Legion's flight. "One with all their gear packed up here to be hauled, and a second hired to recover their pilot from the north?"

"Two pilots," Lyuba replied. "The images show a tandem —front and back—configuration, so something like a radar officer as we have, though not beside you in flight. Presumably more of a navigator and flight engineer here, as the pilot is likely to have his hands completely full with an experimental rocket space plane at impossible speeds, while someone will have to monitor all the other things."

Sasha nodded. The reports had suggested several times the speed of sound. And altitudes that were frankly frightening to contemplate, save that his entire lifetime had seen an equally impossible advancement in aviation technology. Mostly from the many wars, but nonetheless it had still been less than fifty years since the first powered flight. Gennadi's lifetime.

How soon until someone made it fully into space and lived there, like all those silly American radio dramas and books?

There, then, was the future that the Red Branch had to secure for mankind. All mankind. To create enough space that everyone did not have to fight. Could cooperate somehow, just as the Soviet Union and the Western powers had done so recently.

He had to stop the next war from breaking out.

"How well will it fly?" he asked her.

"Depending on their flight envelope, control surfaces, and intended distance, I imagine they will be trying to get the launcher up to something like three to four times gravity acceleration," she nodded. "Enough that the ramjets could fire and push even more, possibly drawing fuel from the launching train itself before disconnecting. From there, separation becomes a matter of letting go as the lifting surfaces will be practically dragging you into the sky. Firing the onboard rockets will push you up and out harder and faster, even as you lose the launcher and quickly the ramjets will run out of fuel. Still, it will fling you into the sky, where the air grows thin and you can move quickly. At some point, the fuel is exhausted and even the thin air will cause you to slow down, but you still have lifting surfaces as you start to fall and can glide a considerable distance. The original Silver Eagle antipodal bomber design assumed several hops, where the pilot would descend into the thicker air, then use that like a glider to rise again."

Sasha could see it. A track like a rabbit fleeing a hawk across a meadow, bounding. Except that this rabbit could leave little prizes behind as it went, destroying buildings.

He was simply happy that nobody but the Americans had access to atomic weapons right now. How soon until someone could drop a city killer from such a weapon? How soon until automated systems were good enough that the entire Silver Eagle could be a missile instead, launched antipodally and carrying an atomic bomb to strike an enemy city intercontinentally?

Moscow? Leningrad? New York City? Washington D.C.?

Or would the world be safer if everyone had such weapons and could equally threaten one another instead of the Americans maintaining a monopoly? It would be like those American western movies, with two cowboys facing off in the street.

He would not have it.

"Would it fly like a glider instead of a jet?" Vanya asked.

"I believe so," she said. "Except that gliders tend to be delicate and responsive. This would be more like a stalled jet in a nose-down dive, barely responding to input. Voss will have to send one of his best pilots, in any sense. Perhaps the one known as Wolf-3."

Ekkehardt Fischer. Small blond man who reminded Sasha of a golden weasel. And at least as dangerous.

Lyuba was watching him. Vanya as well.

He was the Red Branch. These two were merely his officers, with Yuri back at base and Pavel dead.

He would make the decision.

"Let us pack," he said. "Depart as soon as Oleg can return. Better we were there too early and could perhaps delay or destroy the rocket plane than arrive to watch it fly into the northern skies to wreak its terrible havoc."

They both rose and got to work.

He did the same.

The fuse was burning.

CHAPTER 11

Alois stood in the control tower and rotated slowly, taking it all in, perhaps for the last time. Beside, him Dr. Gerstenberger waited patiently.

"It will be something to miss, Doctor," Alois offered.

"I have never been a fan of South America, commander," the man replied. "You know that."

"I'm sure the Americans or Russians would happily take you in," Alois retorted. "They watch the Horten Brothers like hawks. Herr Tank practically has his own team of dedicated spies, following him around daily like the Pied Piper's children. At least you have some freedom of movement. More importantly, freedom to think."

"And I will have a great deal more soon," Gerstenberger shrugged. "Both on the boat and when we arrive. Johannesburg?"

"For now, Doctor," Alois nodded. "One of the few fully independent countries in Africa. And the new National Party that controls the country is instituting a fully segregated society, keeping the lesser races in their place. As they should be.

Plus, the country has enormous mineral resources available, so they will have wealth to perhaps hire us for a time."

"But not a direct sail?" the man asked.

"No," Alois assured him. "First, we sail north to retrieve Ekke and spend some time literally at sea, so that the Americans cannot find us. Later, we will see who needs the Legion to protect them as Stalin and his flunkies decide to push."

"Will the communists not concentrate on China?" Gerstenberger asked.

Alois waved the man to follow as he headed towards the stairs down. He had seen what he needed up here. Clear skies and a good forecast for several days, though there were fronts in America that he needed to prepare for.

Downstairs, he walked a somewhat meandering path, aware that certain conversations in front of air traffic controllers might be repeated later when spies or secret police came.

And they would. Of that, he had no doubts, which was why the Legion had to disappear, in the dead of night as it were, though they would send one Roman candle north first.

"The Chinese, Gerstenberger?" he asked as they were without listening ears. "The Russians hate them the most. Only because it let Stalin extend his power to the Pacific and claim parts of Manchuria would he ever deal with the Nationalists or the Maoists. They will present as friends for a time, before they fall out over something. China sees all of Siberia as land the Russians took from them, just as Tibet only thinks it will be allowed to be independent until Mao needs to bring it back into the fold."

"War between the communist countries?" The man seemed surprised, but he was an academic. An inventor.

"Power corrupts," Alois assured him. "And evil always

turns on itself in the end. They will fall out over something and we will see wars there. "

"And not in Africa?"

"Ah, those will be wars of liberation and independence from colonialism," Alois shrugged. "Things that will damage the British. The French. The Dutch and the Belgians. All of our old enemies. Perhaps even South America eventually, hurting the Americans. The Russians will seek to rush in and exploit such things, bringing them into direct confrontation with the Americans and their allies."

"Do we wish such a thing?" The doctor was confused. Concerned.

"Lat them bleed," Alois said. "Eventually, I expect that we will have to ally with some Western power, because the Reich is well and truly gone. Germany might not return in my lifetime, and I do not imagine that the Russians will ever withdraw from Prussia itself. Not after driving out all the Germans from their ancestral lands in carving out a new Poland. We must turn and fight the Soviets for the world next."

"Next." Gerstenberger was adamant on that, but would have to be, to be willing to assist Alois and his Legion in such a chore.

"Next," Alois agreed. "In the meantime, they will seek mercenaries to help them fight, so they cannot complain when we arrive for hire. Already, the French have a precedent for such a thing with their long-serving Foreign Legion. This simply adds an aircraft component to such wars. And provides us cover."

"So we are not remaining long in South Africa?" Gerstenberger asked.

Alois shrugged. He might not ever arrive there, depending. Such conversations in public were often for the men around him to report later. Let the American and Russian spies guess wrong and chase him there. Perhaps he could go to French Indochina. Or some other African colony where he might fight communist insurgents. Bomb them. Shoot them.

Destroy them utterly.

Alois didn't care, save that he would be forced to choose repugnant sides soon, as galling as that might be.

The Third Reich had failed, and nothing he had seen in South America suggested a Fourth ever rising to stake a claim, much like the Americans and their Lost Cause Confederacy, a candle sputtering out and dying a century later.

Alois had to face the future. Whatever bitterness it might bring.

"So, Doctor Gerstenberger," he turned the conversation away from the politics of sides. "What new aircraft might you steal or adapt for me, given a month or three on a ship to work?"

He missed his Blackhawks, but they had not necessarily proven their worth, especially against those damnable English Vampires. The older, propellor-driven craft around here were all war surplus. Powerful and dangerous, representing a decade of warfare, but already outdated.

The Jet Age had dawned, and the Werewolf Legion needed to take its place in the firmament of such powers.

CHAPTER 12

Vanya had seen the necessity of it, and worked with Arkadi to refine his skills as a thing they might call a cavalry scout in a mechanized unit. Small team that got out ahead of the main force, seeking the enemy in order to call down artillery, armor, or overwhelming force upon someone.

Arkadi was a natural. A young man from northern Russia who had grown up hunting and fishing in a small village. During the war, he had taken those skills with a rifle and tallied twenty-seven confirmed kills at places like Leningrad and others.

And Vanya knew that Arkadi would have preferred his Mosin–Nagant M1891/30 with 3.5 sniper PU scope, but had grown comfortable with his Winchester Model 70 bolt-action sporting rifle. It even had a slightly better scope.

Today, Vanya and Arkadi led, dressed in greens and browns that let them disappear into the fall brush, rather than the blues that would stand out. He had a pair of binoculars with a special shield on the front to keep sunlight from reflecting and giving away his position. Arkadi had an identical pair, as they were not intending to take any shots at the moment.

Though they could.

Both had their pistols, and Vanya had brought his American Thompson M1A1, the old Tommy Gun of the gangster movies, though the military version that only took the straight magazines instead of the drum. Useful at short ranges, where it could put down a tremendous curtain of fire with significant stopping power, but hardly accurate beyond one hundred meters.

That was what he had Arkadi for, but there should be no shooting today. Or there would be far greater troubles.

Grass to waist high around them. Brush of various kinds above that, largely green with leaves already turning brown as southern autumn fell upon them. Back home, the heat would be oppressive.

Vanya had his kit bag slung, and moved with care, largely following the trail Arkadi was taking, until the man stopped, then crept to the top of a low rise, his hat pulled down tight to break up any silhouette.

Vanya waited for the man to wave him closer, then joined Arkadi and looked down. Not much of a valley below. Perhaps ten meters down, but flat for several kilometers running along a north/south axis.

A runway had been paved and extended, it seemed, with that ubiquitous railroad running next to it on the outside, closer to where Vanya was watching. And the far end had been extended beyond the original base, still fenced and running out and up the side of a flattened hill that would add some two hundred meters of sudden elevation at the end.

Banshee had explained the usefulness of such a ski-jump.

Far across the twin paths, a local air base was busy with propeller aircraft. Mostly surplus American gear heavy on old Thunderbolts, though in a distant hangar he saw a pair of Bell

P-63 Kingcobras that brought a smile to his face. Things he had flown during the war.

"Has anything changed?" Vanya asked, pulling up his lenses and quickly quartering the base.

"Less materials scattered around," Arkadi replied. "Less organized, but also less of it. Packed up what they wanted and leaving the rest?"

"Such I surmise, yes," Vanya replied. "How close are they?"

"Soon, but not today," Arkadi said. "Unless it is an emergency. I see several crates piled up for a forklift to carry to the railroad that is in the far side of the base."

Vanya considered the layout. This side of the base looked to have been added recently, with the railroad newest, emerging from a factory building at the low end, where they no doubt would fuel and assemble the needle. Older barracks and hangars over across the way.

Had the locals not understood what the Werewolf Legion were doing? Or had they fallen into that same rapturous belief that having rocket-powered space planes would suddenly make South America as important as North?

After all, if you could travel from Buenos Aires to Chicago in less than an hour, how much closer was every city on earth? Cargo that used to take weeks might take hours. One could already talk via telephone lines that would soon replace telegraphs.

How soon until the entire world was just next door?

He supposed that some people might let the possibilities of wealth blind them. Look at what had gone wrong with Pavel.

"Oh, that's new," Arkadi murmured.

"What?"

"On the south end, just coming around the building," Arkadi said.

Vanya turned and scowled into his lenses as an American tank, a Sherman M4A3E8, the so-called Easy Eight that represented the final version of one of their best vehicles of the war. Long-barrel 76mm cannon. Extra armor. Better engines.

Exactly not the sort of base defenses Vanya would like to have to deal with, were it necessary to attack the place. This on top of the Oerlikon cannons on corners and rooftops, as though someone had whispered in their ears that *Banshee* would be coming for them again.

The Sherman circled the south end of the runway and railroad as he watched, coming to rest almost below them inside the wire, facing out about midway between ends where it could quickly react to any trouble with machine guns and main cannon.

"What does it mean, Vanya?" Arkadi asked.

"They grow close," he said. "Someone has decided that they are moving forward shortly and called for anyone who could to support them with enough firepower to protect the base."

"We still need to sneak in and stop them, correct?" Arkadi asked. "I am certain that I could shoot the railcar and the rocket, perhaps damaging them enough to explode. The range is not that bad if I had time to bring up a rest and settle."

"And it may come to that," Vanya said. "For now, let us memorize everything that has changed, so we can brief Sasha and the others. I suspect that they will be moving in tonight, if our wolf friends are so nervous that they have brought in the Paraguayan army to assist."

He settled in and scanned the base once, then pulled out maps he had sketched from photographs and started adding details. Machine gun nests. Anti-aircraft batteries. That tank. A set of armored cars parked on the other side of the distant fence, but presumably available in an emergency and capable of destroying anything less than the Sherman with their smaller guns, while being largely immune to what the Red Branch normally carried.

Did they need to add a heavy weapons team at some point? Mortars? Machine guns? Rockets?

He had expected a life in the air, fighting other pilots and mercenaries, but Vanya could see where things had already escalated far beyond that.

How far?

CHAPTER 13

Sasha watched the sun set and hoped it was not a metaphor.

Below, the Legion base had not missed a single beat in operations, according to Arkadi, who had been left in place all afternoon while Vanya had withdrawn to bring in the team. Lights on tall poles kept most of the facility as clear as day.

At least on this side.

On the Army side, things were darker. Normal, as it were, when there were no alerts and no expectation of aircraft able to launch on thirty seconds notice when a radar operator has spotted a massed air armada approaching.

Thus, Sasha was confident that the Paraguayans were not expecting trouble. And Voss hadn't bothered letting them know that it might be coming, but Sasha could almost smell it in the air, like smoke on a distant breeze.

He laid flat next to Arkadi and watched, comparing what he saw to what Vanya had mapped and explained before the stalk.

They had left the trucks several miles away, then followed a dry ravine and several game trails that he would have missed, save that Vanya had mentioned his new job as a cavalry scout to explain.

All of them were growing and changing as necessary in this new world.

Sasha turned to Vanya on his far side.

"That tank keeps the hatch closed," he noted. "There is no way to harm it thus, is there?"

"Short of opening the hatch from the outside and shooting in or dropping a grenade we didn't have with us, no," Vanya replied. "We will need to expand our abilities."

Sasha added it to the list. He had originally intended to create what the Germans had once called their flying circus under Richthofen, all bright colors and spectacular pilots.

Circumstances were turning him into a commando operation. Fortunately, he had many of the right people already.

He turned to Ilya and waved the man close, gesturing Vanya to withdraw for now.

"Sir?"

Sasha pointed.

"Both teams need to get inside the wire," Sasha said simply. "How and where?"

Ilya had trained in underwater demolitions. One of the hardest and least forgiving tasks in a war, because even the environment could kill you without noticing. Like Arkadi, it taught stealth, but amplified that because Ilya's people had to touch their target to place explosives, rather than stand off at a distance and shoot it from relative safety.

Ilya watched, eyes quartering things right to left quickly and nodding.

"The Legion is too alert," he finally said. "We need to enter from the Paraguayan side, steal some uniforms, and Red-2 needs a jeep that lets him get close to the tank."

"What would he do to the tank?" Sasha asked, intrigued.

"Order them to open the hatch, then take them prisoner," Ilya chuckled. "Or just shoot them, depending. That tank is an irresistible force on this battleground, assuming that the Oerlikon cannon cannot be depressed to bear inside the wire, which they should not be allowed to for safety reasons. Not even the armored cars are a match. That also allows him to hide and watch safely from extremely close in."

Sasha nodded. Expertise was why he had hired all of these people. Killers with war experience against the Nazis. And brains.

While there were times when charging a machine gun nest was the only solution, Sasha preferred men and women who would think their way around such trouble and take it in a flank.

Speaking of which...

He turned to Lyuba and shifted so she could slide in beside him as he waved her close.

"You and I," he said, nodding to the base. "Ilya, Oleg, and Nikon. Vanya as team two, with Arkadi and Yanina, following close, but not in the direct line. We need inside the facility to see how we can stop them, because merely damaging the rails or the Silver Eagle only delays things. They must be stopped."

She nodded.

"Nikon, I will need you to take some prisoners for their uniforms," she said simply to the man. "I can remain in these brown fatigues, or change back to blue, because they are not prepared to encounter any woman in any uniform. We will use that as a weapon. The rest of you need to become Paraguayan Air Corps. When do we strike?"

That last, looking at him.

Sasha turned to the south end of things. Darkness, because

the base was well away from any of the neighboring villages, connected only by electric lines back to civilization.

For a moment, he considered what might happen if someone took out a power pole, but again, that only delayed the inevitable. It did not stop the Legion. Might instead cause them to race madly ahead with their preparations, feeling the hangman's noose descending upon them.

"Now," he decided. "Arkadi, get us around to a place where you and Ilya can get us inside without alarms."

Both men nodded and Sasha slid backwards, pausing to wipe dust off his tan jacket as they moved deeper into a deepening darkness uncut by moonlight.

The new moon had set with the sun, drawing everything into darkness.

Save what light he could bring to the world.

CHAPTER 14

Arkadi stalked the most dangerous game. Even the wolves of his homeland knew to flee a man with a rifle, but he was about to go into the den of a violent creature and hurt it.

Fortunately, the Paraguayan military could not hold a candle to the Nazis he'd stalked. Nor the Soviets he had protected.

Ilya let him lead. That one was good when you got in close, but this was yet wilderness to be penetrated. Brush and cover to be taken advantage of to get a small team of killers close enough for a man like Ilya to work.

Game trails, where the locals had not developed the habits of actually walking armed patrols outside the wire to prevent someone doing exactly what Arkadi did now. Instead, they relied on cyclone fencing and barbed wire, defining a spot to keep out wildlife larger than a rabbit.

Dogs or geese would have been smart, but he had seen nothing along those lines in his scope. Only men. Nightblind because the Legion base was lit any time someone looked to the east and the guards would be too stupid to permanently turn their backs on that side.

At the other Legion base, there had been a ravine that let them in, because such things disrupted continuity. Arkadi had seen similar things here. More drainage than a creek that provided fresh water, but no one had bothered to dig drainage pipes deep under ground here. Smart, he supposed, when the rains were not that intense most of the time. You needed the ability to quickly wash off the heaviest flash, but it wasn't an ongoing deluge.

Deserts and drylands, flashflooded and gone.

Still, someone had at least enough of an idea to register. Arkadi found a creek bed as they circled, then followed it back uphill to where a two-meter pipe emerged from a concrete basin.

From memory, it pointed back to the Paraguayan side of the base. The older section. He supposed that there might be a spur, somewhere deep inside and newer, that ran to the Legion section, but they would have to gain access to know.

Turning, he waved everyone down, then gestured Ilya to follow.

"No, take Nikon," Ilya whispered.

Arkadi shrugged and the man with the Chinese *Tang Hands* training joined him as they moved into the ditch and along the bank. There was the faintest dribble of water tonight. Hardly enough to matter, save that it showed a connection to some source inside the base.

A way in. That was what he needed.

Arkadi led them onto the slab where they water emerged from the hole and fell, eyes up along the higher ground ahead of him. Base ground level, where he was beneath them.

"Nikon?" he murmured.

The man stepped up and shined a pencil light into the hole for a long moment, grunting.

"Large enough to walk," he said. "Though Yuri would be bitching constantly."

Arkadi chuckled. Most Soviets were small. Poor nutrition and a lifetime of war. Red-5 was a Russian Bear. Or a Ukrainian one, anyway.

"Will it work for you?" Arkadi asked.

"Yes," Nikon said. "Ilya will lead, with me immediately behind protecting him and the first team. You will trail the second team, covering our rear until we split and fork our attacks."

"You think we will take the tank?" Arkadi asked.

Not impossible. Difficult to do without too many people asking too many questions, at a time when any mistake might kill them all.

"I think the Commissar can," Nikon nodded. "It provides a base to retreat from, as well, shooting back. Unless you can get up on the roof as a roost, there are precious few other options, and most of those leave you strung out as a pennant in the wind when everything goes wrong."

Arkadi accepted that. Snipers were often forced into awkward positions to make a shot. It would be worse with two others close, even if both could move silently.

But a tank changed many equations.

He would let Vanya decide.

"You wait here," Nikon ordered. "I will go get the others."

CHAPTER 15

Ilya was used to close quarters, where the enemy might be no more than a few meters away, unknowing that death stalked them. Unlike Arkadi, striking from a distance, Ilya had to get close enough to plant bombs. Sometimes, that involved holding his breath as he swam under black waters to attach a mine, like that one German E-boat.

Memory made him smile.

Here, he walked with his eyes down, confident that Nikon and that rochin in one hand protected him.

Ilya was watching for traps, as unexpected as they might be. Wires that he might trip over. Something.

During the war, the Nazis had grown extremely competent about such things, after initial complacency that had cost them dearly. The survivors had, anyway.

Additionally, he paced his steps with care, knowing exactly where he was on a map if it became necessary, because sometimes you planted a bomb in a mine and let the earth above you damage the target in erupting.

The outer wire had not been that far from the nearest barracks on this side, unlike the more spacious areas of the

Legion base, but they only needed barracks for a few, hangars, and that one factory in the middle that was making the devilbird.

His light found a square spot on one side. Ilya paused Nikon to look up at metal bars set as a ladder into the concrete, thence to a manhole cover overhead.

He signaled the commander close.

"We are under the main quad outside the barracks here, sir," Ilya said. "We could surface here and penetrate."

"We don't need prisoners," Nikon offered. "Merely uniforms. Where would the laundry be?"

Ilya paused on that novel concept. That water would go down different drains, as Arkadi had mentioned this as more of a storm overflow designed to keep runways dry, but it should pass directly under the building, and possibly several others. Would there be a spot inside the building?

Doubtful. Even the locals wouldn't be stupid enough to let someone break into their building this way, would they?

"Possibly a laundry here," Ilya shrugged. "Or a storage building for the quartermaster, closer to officer's quarters where blackmarketeers could not so easily get at things."

"Can you pick the lock?" the commander asked.

"Easily, if there are not people watching," Ilya replied.

"Go deeper," Sasha ordered. "A supply warehouse likely means fewer people and more alternatives."

Ilya nodded and got back into motion.

Another hundred meters and he was under the area close to the motor pool. He found a ladder and pointed. Nikon went up immediately, shifting the cover quietly and sticking his head up. Darkness, so no internal lights flooded the area.

Not yet, anyway. An alarm would not doubt change that.

"Warehouse, motor pool, command barracks, and possibly

armory, sir," Nikon reported when he dropped down. "Area five on Vanya's map."

Yes. Ilya grinned. Right where he thought.

The commander matched his smile.

"You two, to the surface and into the warehouse," he ordered. "Uniforms for everyone first priority, regardless of fit for now. That lets us move around more freely before we hit the motor pool."

"Motor pool?" Nikon asked.

"Vanya's team will need to steal a jeep," the commander chuckled.

Ilya joined him.

Now, to work.

CHAPTER 16

Nikon crept out of the hole, standing and waiting for Ilya to join him a moment later. The lights from the Legion base cast deep shadows here, so the hole was merely a deeper darkness, even as the commander's head emerged with a pistol barrel.

Nikon kept his rochin up under his arm like a swagger stick for now. Out of sight but available to block or stab.

It was really a length of wood, turned to about three centimeters diameter and split at one end for a flat piece of steel that had been mounted on bolts and sharpened in a diamond shape. Not a sword, but able to slash and stab equally. Okinawan, originally, but those islands shared many martial arts with the Chinese mainland historically, and had carried the Tang Hand to Japan in the early part of the century under Funikoshi and his students.

Nikon had been exposed to many things from the comrades, during his time helping train them in Soviet equipment and tactics. Some of those arts went back centuries, and used any number of odd and exotic weapons he had come to appreciate. The rochin was still among his favorite, because it was a club when he needed and killing blade otherwise.

Here, he could block and strike equally, then flow to open hands or kicks as needed, but few of the Chinese arts could drop a man as quickly. Or efficiently.

Ilya moved like his shadow, getting to the warehouse building door. It had a small light over it, but mostly to show you where it was in the dark. Or let someone standing outside for a smoke see.

Nikon walked right up and leaned back against the wall with a foot up, like a man dragging on a cigarette and no cares in the world. Distraction. Enough to draw the eye to him, lest someone ask why Ilya was kneeling at the door and fussing with it.

Not that the man needed long.

"Cheap lock," Ilya grumbled, almost bouncing as quickly as he rose again.

They entered into a vast space only sparsely lit. Nikon listened with senses that went beyond the ears, but there was nobody about. Stacks of shelves in every direction, with greater space on the left that felt like where a railroad car could be pushed inside to be unloaded by overhead cranes.

Offices on the right, all dark.

Nikon watched Ilya wave to the commander, then they went deeper, towards those offices.

All were locked. He watched Sasha, *Banshee*, and Oleg appear at the outer door and close it silently as Ilya opened them one at a time.

"Here," Ilya said on the third one.

Nikon looked in. Shelves as outside, but uniforms in all sizes. Many looked American surplus, things he had worn in the war when all the factories had either been destroyed, or dismantled to haul off beyond the Urals to keep them out of reach of Nazi bombers and tank legions.

They all wore brown tonight, so adding a green jacket was enough, at least to get close. The dark would mask many sins until it was too late for someone to raise an alarm.

Sasha got them changed, then grabbed full uniforms for the other three. Nikon took Oleg with him and they quickly scouted the rest of the warehouse, as Oleg could disappear into any role and confuse something, were they to suddenly meet.

Ilya would kill them so fast they missed it.

Space indeed where rail cars could be drawn in and emptied. Other spaces where trucks could be backed up onto a dock and unloaded. Garage doors in many places. Personnel doors in others. Everything closed and locked when he touched them, just to make sure.

They were in the middle of small air corps base. Probably several hundred airmen around them, though not that professional. And all the pilots were just across the way, possibly still up drinking, though he had heard no noise indicating a party ongoing.

The mechanics were not having to work late tonight to get aircraft ready for flight at false dawn, and that was all Nikon cared about.

He got Oleg back to the others, just as the Commissar and his two assistants got changed into proper uniforms.

"Now what?" he heard *Banshee* asking.

Sasha looked around at the group with the sort of deadly seriousness that Nikon remembered from that one old man on a dojo floor in the Chinese mountains.

"Now, we must go save the world," Sasha told them.

Nikon shivered in spite of himself.

CHAPTER 17

Sasha stepped close to Vanya, keeping his voice low in spite of Nikon assuring him that the facility was empty.

"A jeep driving around now will likely cause someone to ask questions," he said. "But you should move there and be prepared. You intend to simply roll up and issue orders?"

"Unless someone has given them specific instructions, I cannot imagine that they would open fire indiscriminately, Sasha," he replied. "More likely they are mostly sitting around bored. Possibly one sergeant awake and one of the men, and the other three sleeping or playing cards. Ready for an alert, should one come, but not *prepared*."

Sasha nodded. It made a certain sense. He had learned a new term while in South America.

Mañana.

Tomorrow.

I will get to it tomorrow.

Or not.

There was a certain, cultural lassitude that this former New Soviet Man simply did not understand, but they could take advantage of it while they were here.

"So you and your team will be ready to go?" Sasha asked, glancing at Arkadi and Yanina.

"I can drive a Sherman tank, commander," Yanina smiled.

He gawked for a moment, then nodded.

They had all had to do whatever had been necessary to stop the Nazis from conquering the world. And the Party had rewarded them.

If you could call it that.

They were here.

"What would you do with a stolen tank?" he asked, mostly curious but it was Vanya.

"Inflict chaos as necessary," Vanya replied evenly. "If the Legion is mostly packed, one would presume that they would be more likely to simply jump in trucks and flee, rather than fight to the death. Especially if some maniac in a tank is parked on the runway and threatening to blow up any aircraft attempting to take off."

His smile was terrible, but Sasha had spoken with Gennadi about the man. *The Commissar.*

Cool under all circumstances. Almost coldly logical that way.

A man willing to do the thing that must be done. Regardless of the personal costs.

Sounded like someone else Sasha knew.

"Make sure you get away safely later," Sasha reminded him, turning to Arkadi and Yanina to intervene if necessary.

He had lost Pavel, but that had been to evil. Sasha had no interest in losing more people. Especially not the ones that had begun to turn into friends.

"Indeed," Vanya said, then drew his two off towards the main door that would let him slip into the nearby motor pool.

That left Sasha with his inner core of a commando unit.

"There are too many lights on, in the Legion side of the base," he said simply. "And the wire in place between us. I fear that they are staying up all night to do something, so we must move."

"Can they launch in the darkness?" Ilya asked.

"The space plane moves too quickly," Lyuba replied. "They will be to New York City in as little as an hour, moving incredibly rapidly. I would want to have sunlight to assist my bombing run. I expect them to launch just as dawn comes over the horizon here."

Sasha nodded. Several hours left to intervene, however they would.

Whatever they needed to do.

He turned to Ilya.

"How do we do this?" he asked.

"Back underground, sir," his sidekick replied. "There will be another pipe that crosses over."

"Go find it," Sasha ordered, falling into the middle as Ilya and Nikon moved.

Time was running short.

CHAPTER 18

Lyuba walked in the tunnel behind Sasha, with Oleg behind her. She kept her pistol holstered for now, somewhat covered by the green American jacket that she wore for a disguise. It was difficult to see anything around the much taller Sasha, but lights showed the tunnel continuing.

Then everything stopped.

"Lateral pipe, sir," Ilya announced quietly.

"Go," Sasha replied, and they were headed roughly east.

If the map in her head matched the ground, they were headed towards that new factory building that held the Legion. Where the spies had mentioned building and perfecting a Silver Eagle antipodal bomber.

A sub-orbital terror weapon, because it was not a proper tool of war.

But how soon until someone could put a small base permanently into orbit like a naval vessel, filled with bombs that could be dropped on cities? How soon until universal terror was the human condition, as the sky was a threat at all times?

Or would the next war simply destroy so much that nobody ever escaped the sky?

She did not like where these thoughts took her, but there was little Lyuba could do about it. Technology was a terrible mistress in service to warfare.

And human greed.

She had no doubts that the Nazis of the Werewolf Legion were clear out at the cutting edge of science and aeronautical engineering with what they were doing. Had they merely sought to invent new tools, the Americans might have even welcomed them, like they had with so many others.

Instead, they were wallowing in their evil.

And one did not negotiate with evil.

One destroyed it. If they had truly built a Silver Eagle, the Werewolf Legion needed to be eradicated from the face of the earth.

And the heavens.

Time passed as they progressed up the new tunnel. Overhead, they had crossed the wire into the Legion's kennel, and would be soon under the factory.

Ilya stopped at another ladder.

"We might be inside," he murmured. "Or just outside. It is hard to tell because of the geometry of that angle."

She watched Nikon ascend. Heard the faintest sound as the man lifted the cover and moved it, stronger than the wiry man he appeared. Sasha moved halfway up the ladder, then returned a moment later.

"Inside," he told the group simply. "Behind some crates and shelves, so move carefully. I did not see anyone, but could hear them moving around."

Lyuba nodded.

There were no women known in the Werewolf Legion, according to all the information anyone had been able to compile. She had the job with the Red Branch because she was an expert at aeronautical engineering and low-level attack.

Anyone she encountered would be immediately suspicious of a woman.

She would have to tailor those suspicions.

"Hold," she said, then proceeded to strip off her top layers until she had only her bra, before putting the jacket back on and not the underlayers.

It gave her cleavage and exposed skin to distract. She supposed that she could have gone farther, perhaps no bra and only one jacket button hooked, such that she was at risk of falling out, but any woman would distract in this situation.

And her blonde hair would not fit with any idea of a local prostitute that someone might have snuck onto the base. They would be darker in skin and hair. And furtive.

She was a killer.

Sasha watched her without comment, but he had seen her in far less. The men were all professionals, though she could tell that she had shocked even them.

Good.

Her job as wingman was to distract from the main body of killers around her. And she could always injure a man too surprised to resist.

Men had so many soft and fragile spots.

"You are certain?" Sasha asked.

"I will confuse them more than a random stranger walking around," Lyuba replied. "Especially the uniform. Perhaps someone brought a girlfriend onto the base and put her in his uniform to hide her. Perhaps someone brought a prostitute. Something. It buys you time to react."

She turned to Nikon, with his deadly hands.

"You will protect me," she intoned.

His nod was precise, tight, and lethal. Eyes that promised a terrible reckoning.

All these men would protect her, like their goddess come to earth. Only Pavel had ever looked down on her a *mere woman*.

She was so much more. And the Werewolf Legion was about to discover that.

"*Banshee* and Nikon lead," Sasha said. "Ilya, watch for places to inflict destruction. Oleg, on one flank in the role of a confused, Paraguayan airman who needs to also distract anyone he encounters. We are scouting the facility to see where they are at and how much time we have to stop them. If need be, we will simply attack and damn the consequences, but that is a third option at present. Questions?"

Lyuba nodded. That encapsulated things.

They would do what they had to do to stop the Legion.

Whatever it took to save the sky.

CHAPTER 19

Alois lit another cigarette and watched the entire affair from the safety of his upstairs office. Through the plate glass window keeping smells at bay. With all of the factory spread out below him.

With his other hand, he grabbed his coffee mug, noticed it was empty, and moved to where someone had brewed a fresh pot on a side table.

Patience was not his strong suit this evening.

He sucked a lungful of smoke and blew it out, thankful that they had installed several series of venting fans in the roof when they had moved in, able to draw out all fumes before they could accumulate and pose any sort of spark risk.

Below, Wolf-2 supervised a team fueling the Silver Eagle for its maiden voyage into history. Touchy stuff, the rocket fuel that Gerstenberger had come up with. Possibly an invention worthy of a Nobel Prize, were the formulation made public at some point.

Alois had no time for Buck Rogers dreams of fantastic space adventures.

He turned to Gerstenberger anyway, seated at the table in

the middle of the room. The man was oblivious, busy running some calculations that appeared to fill at least one page. Rather than interrupt, Alois returned to the window and watched his wolves work.

In addition to his pilots and radarmen, Alois had brought most of the ground team he had hired in Argentina, an even mix of escaped fascists and ambitious locals willing to accept loyalty to his dreams, Buck Rogers or not.

Another drag on the cigarette. The smoke calmed him. Some. Perhaps enough.

Perhaps not.

The door opened and his hand strayed to the pistol on his hip, but only a flinch. Only for a flinch. Enough to betray his nerves.

Giving up the dreams of the Reich was harder than he had imagined.

And yet, tomorrow raced ever closer, and brought forth that ever-deadly *day-after*, when he would be forced to pick the poison that he would drink.

The Americans, or the Soviets.

Not that it was much of a choice. Nor that there would be much doubt.

That wouldn't make the taste any better.

Ekke had paused in the doorway for an equal blink, then entered, with Lars on his heels. Gerstenberger looked up, then put aside his current project and waved them close.

Alois joined them at the table as Herr Doctor rose and spread out a map.

The American eastern seaboard, from North Carolina to Hudson Bay, marked with all those lovely spots that Alois would have loved to annihilate, had he a dozen Silver Eagles at his disposal today, instead of the one.

"The weather holds," Gerstenberger announced, pulling out several other documents that had been telegraphed from the north. "Dry and generally warm across the entire eastern half of the United States. For Americans, a glorious summer day. Even the Canadians might venture outside to enjoy it, but we presume that they might catch fire in sunlight."

Alois shared the laughter. The Americans had been a dangerous, deadly giant in the war, but Hitler had always worried more about the Canadian army. For all their small size, they had always punched well above their weight, to use a boxing image.

Hockey players, woodsmen, and Mounties. Generally friendly enough, though, even if their wrath had been terrible. Let them rage inconsequentially tomorrow, when he escaped.

At least, after Ekke was safely aboard a ship already quietly waiting in Hudson Bay and preparing to rescue these two men.

Assuming that they survived.

Alois had lost count of all the ways that this project could go wrong. And most of them were lethal. Even the little ones ended with Ekke and Lars having to bail out at high altitude, trusting their experimental flight suits to keep them alive as they parachuted down to wherever they might land.

Gerstenberger assumed that any mistake in flight ended in a sudden fireball that lit up the entire seaboard.

Alois turned to Wolf-3.

"You have your papers?" he asked the two men.

Both reached into messenger bags and pulled out wallets, opening them to show documents and cash that would let them hide as Americans if they came down early.

And alive.

"Survival gear?" he continued.

"Sigie is storing them with the parachutes, to be loaded

when he completes fueling," Ekke replied evenly. "Maps, firearms, food for a few days, plus general hiking gear if we need to survive outdoors. There is an inflatable raft as well."

Alois knew that his nerves were causing him to go over everything in excruciating detail, after his team had already done this several times and assembled everything they could think of for Wolf-3 to survive.

Except luck, but Ekke brought his own to the table.

Alois checked his watch. Paused to wind it on general principles, because today was not the day for it to run down. Sucked down the last of his cigarette while he did so, then crushed it out atop a bed of similar corpses in the ashtray.

"What remains?" he asked, looking at the two men.

"Lars and I will have dinner in a bit," Ekke replied. "The mess hall is staying up late to fix us steak and eggs. Then a brief nap because it has been a long day and tomorrow will be even more exciting. In a few hours we will insert into the Silver Eagle, be locked inside, and you will roll us around outside where we can count down to dawn."

Alois noted the shark-like smile on Lars's face. The man hardly ever spoke, confident that Wolf-3 would have said it. He merely nodded now. Alois matched it.

"Then go get ready," he ordered them. "Tomorrow, we shall enter the history books, gentlemen."

They shook hands round-robin, then departed. Gerstenberger settled back in his chair and did whatever maths he had been preoccupied with.

Alois returned to the window and lit another cigarette.

CHAPTER 20

Sigmar Schmidt dreamed about the War.

Bombing and strafing the British and French fleeing to Dunkirk as Wolf-2 had done. Duels over eastern England, before his Fuhrer had pulled back from the infamous Battle of Britain. Operation Barbarossa.

They had come so close to wiping out the Slavs. To opening all of Siberia to *Lebensraum*.

Today, he was a fugitive in South America, hiding from those same scum.

Sigmar watched the ground crew go over their checklists with triple redundant detail. One man calling out a step. Two others confirming as it was done.

Mostly, it was the fuel that had everyone on edge. Experimental stuff. Extremely dangerous.

Alois had forbidden anyone from smoking tonight for any reason, then gone upstairs into his lair because he needed to anyway. Sigmar would simply beat someone to death right now for even having a lighter in a pocket, but that was his own nerves at the process.

An awful lot of volatile fuel being slowly pumped into the

tanks of the Silver Eagle first, then the railcar that was its cradle. And two full teams of fire fighters, standing around with nothing at all to do unless and until something went wrong.

Sigmar intended nothing to go wrong. Still, one team with charged hoses, ready to spray water on anything to cool it. Another team with fire extinguisher canisters, charged and ready to swoop in.

Patience was the only thing keeping his nerves stable.

At the same time, being in command of this operation meant that he had nothing to do with his hands, so Sigmar moved over to where the pumps were working.

"Status?" he asked gruffly.

"Three quarters full now, sir," the man replied. "Another thirty minutes here, then we'll move on to the main tank. That's about two hours, as we only need to top those tanks off."

Sigmar nodded. Sighed, but only inside.

Wolf-4 and Wolf-6 continued watching and supervising, so he moved around to the front of the Silver Eagle, imagining what it would look like, piercing the sky like an arrow.

Flat underbelly with a heat shield for the immense temperatures that would be generated. Stubby wings front and back in a double tandem like darts one might use in a bar.

It was not silver, but a basic gray paint that was also heat resistant and smooth to reduce friction. Still, it would be a bolt of lightning from the blue.

He moved to a table nearby and confirmed that the landing gear had all been removed from the craft, left here out of the way as a visual reminder because it would not be needed.

Once Ekke launched, the craft would never land again. Merely slam into the ground at high speed and disintegrate.

Or detonate in the air when something went wrong.

He hoped it would be sudden and complete, if it came to that. Sigmar could think of nothing worse than to be trapped inside a burning aircraft taking minutes to plummet out of the sky while you watched helplessly.

He had seen too many of his friends go that way at the end, after doing it to the Russians first.

Content, he walked over and touched the underbelly of the Eagle on the nearer wing, where the landing gear cover was closed and bolted into place permanently.

Slowly, he completed his latest loop, aware that after having done it this many times it probably qualified as a nervous tic. Sigmar was okay with that.

Nobody had ever done something like this. Even von Braun's people had only invented short-range ballistic missiles to strike London, rather than something that could have annihilated Stalin's Moscow after Barbarossa had failed and Bagration had trapped the Wehrmacht between the Americans and the Russians.

Then annihilated it in the worst loss the army had ever seen, when all Sigmar had been able to do had been to fly overhead and try to stop the onslaught.

Like holding back the tide.

Hopefully, Alois would take them to Africa or the Middle East, one of these days, so they could rain Silver Eagle fire down on Moscow. Leningrad. Stalingrad. Yekaterinburg. Vladivostok.

Every Russian city, consumed in purifying fires.

And purified as the Mongols might have done it.

Sigmar went back to the checklists and checked his watch.

CHAPTER 21

Sasha followed Ilya, with the rest of the team back and off to the sides holding flanks against surprises.

The last thing he needed was a firefight inside a building. Especially when the Legion was busy fueling their rocket plane for the attack. Sasha imagined that the explosion would gut the building and possibly level it, killing half the people inside.

It had always amazed him, to see people emerge from bombed buildings, sometimes without a scratch. The British had gone into the War with an expectation that their Strategic Bombing campaigns could cripple or neutralize any threat, but hadn't understood how stupid that was until they'd been on the receiving end of the Blitz.

People were far more resilient than planners or generals ever imagined.

The facility was huge. Several hectares under roof, divided into various components separated by barn doors.

They had entered from the north-west corner, about as far from the current activities as possible, but Sasha appreciated the ability to move around without encountering people. He was back to that first time with Yuri, in Argentina, scouting the

Werewolf Legion's factory assembling those Blackhawk fighters.

Here, there were machining bays for making parts, but not nearly as much space. Estimates had suggested that Voss's space plane was a little longer than twenty meters, with a span just over ten. Not a lot of materials to fabricate, but they were working in exotic alloys, so there were heavy presses and tools necessary to shape such things.

And they had to happen here, on site, because one could not order the pieces of a space plane from some catalog.

The air held a faint whiff of sharpness he associated with their rocket fuel, though whole banks of fans overhead pulled any vapors up and away, so there was less risk of a spark igniting everything.

It also covered any sound he wanted to make, because those things tended to be loud. Sasha could still shout over them if he wanted, but could talk close to Ilya without someone hearing.

Ilya had moved to a corner and peeked around. The man waved Sasha close.

They looked.

Sasha could see the Eagle in the distance, in another section of the factory through the distant open barn doors between them. On the right, at an even greater distance, he saw an office overlooking the space, like he had once seen on an American aircraft carrier where the Air Boss commanded the flight wing.

A figure in the window that he suspected was Voss, but the distance was too great to make out more than the silhouette of a man. Sasha watched him turn away as lights spilling out indicated a door opening. Two figures entered the office, then the door closed.

"Watch that space," Sasha ordered Ilya, then gestured Lyuba close.

"Voss," he said, pointing. "That might be where he is running things from."

"Do we destroy it?" she asked.

Sasha shook his head. Lopping the head off of that snake might help, but he needed to make it a clean sweep if they initiated violence in here.

When.

Even getting out alive later was not necessarily the first priority, if it meant that the Legion was destroyed in the process.

"Watch them and see what Voss is doing," he told her, leaning in to her ear. "Two men just entered."

Her eyes took on a hard glint.

"Were those the pilots of the Eagle, having one last check-in?" she asked.

Sasha considered it. They had been assuming that all of the efforts in the main barn would be dedicated towards a dawn launch, but what if they were wrong?

What if Voss intended to bomb New York City in the dead of night?

He could not afford to guess wrong. Not as big as any mistake might be.

"Let us find out," he told her, then tapped Ilya. "Get us to Voss's office so that we can identify who he meets with."

Ilya was used to German tactics and mindset, so he immediately backed them up and around as Sasha watched, quickly crossing laterally to another barn door, this section entirely dark. Not even overhead lights turned down.

They were in time, though, as Sasha saw that same staircase door open, spilling light on the outside wall, then two men descending.

From the darkness, he could identify the first man as Ekkehardt Fischer. Wolf-3. That presumed the man following was his radarman, Lars Weber.

Given all the Werewolves to fly that space plane, Sasha felt like Voss would send that man. Wolf-2 was another option, but he had been seen supervising the fueling of the plane. And other Wolves had been doing various tasks, everyone intently watching inward to the point that Sasha wondered how close he could have gotten.

Except that such a move would have simply caused a firefight in the middle of a fuel depot.

And an explosion large enough that it might be visible from Asuncion.

There were still other war criminals out there to hunt.

Fischer and his wingmate moved to the bottom of the ladder, then exited the building.

"After them," Sasha prodded Ilya and Nikon into motion. "We will follow you slower."

Because he needed to track Fischer immediately.

The fate of the world might depend on it.

CHAPTER 22

Ilya was back in Königsberg, haunting that one Nazi naval base that sent E-boats out into the Baltic as hunters. Time had been critical, more than once, getting in or out while dressed in Nazi gray for long enough to confuse a guard.

Whatever it took to get too close to be stopped, whether that was a knife in a kidney or a grenade into the back of a truck driving away.

Nikon had trained on other things, but moved quickly in total silence, so Ilya focused on crossing the darkness to an outside door he remembered from photographs, hoping that the floor underfoot would be flat, paved, and that nothing to trip over had been left out.

Somewhere behind, the Major would bring along the others. Or perhaps keep watch on the bird while he and Nikon stalked. It had been two men, down a staircase in semi-darkness, then turn back and out through a door.

Where were they going at this time of night, if everyone else was focused on the bomber? Ilya let that worry goad his feet faster, until they got to the end of the current aisle and he found the door. Unlocked, so he silently opened it a crack and peeked out.

Open courtyard. Barracks building across the way, only partly lit and that part the ground floor on the right.

Smells. Ah, food. The canteen is open and feeding the crew.

He just managed to catch the second shadow as the man entered the barracks building and closed the door, leaving open windows to spill light and fried potatoes into the night.

Ilya considered the layout. Open space, so anyone moving might be seen, but badly lit, because the outside lights were either off or only one in four running.

"You wait here for the Major," he whispered to Nikon.

It was unfortunate, splitting, but they had forked the road and Ilya needed to be closer. Extremely close. Toss a grenade in as you drive by close.

Nikon nodded and held back. Ilya stood up and tugged at his jacket, then walked directly across the space like he belonged here, tending to his right as though entering the barracks instead of the canteen. If he had done the math correctly.

Darkness. He had not counted how many men had been servicing the bomber, but it had been many. And focused. Men with deadly intent, working under the close supervision of officers that had no sense of humor.

Nazi. Or Commissars, if Vanya was having a bad day, few though those were.

Men not given to horseplay. Busy.

He found the other door into the barracks. Away from the offices and canteen. Hopefully, where pilots could come and go to the factory as they needed.

Unlocked.

He pulled the door open and stepped inside with a knife hidden in one hand. Back to Königsberg.

Nobody confronted him.

Hallway. Tiled. Gypsum board walls painted a dingy mustard. Fluorescent lights overhead with a tinny buzzing that had to be aggravating if one spent to much time indoors.

Ilya walked like a man on an errand. Not stern, but not meandering like a thief, either.

Königsberg.

Fortunately, there was nobody about. Doors closed, with signs marking occupancy, so he paused and counted, memorizing names against a list Sasha had provided at one point.

Voss, Schmidt, and Fischer were not here. Nor was Gerstenberger. Names like Weber, Wagner, Schulz, and Bauer, so he was in the area allocated to the enlisted men like him.

Pilots officers would be elsewhere. Ilya went deeper into the building. At the far end of the hallway, he could see another exit door that would get him outside and perhaps close to where Vanya and his team waited for whatever alarm might be raised. Ilya hit the center of the building and looked all four ways, continuing forward and finding where the Nazi scientist Gerstenberger had his rooms.

Locked, and Ilya didn't want to be seen breaking in, so he memorized the location and went back to the central axis, moving laterally now as he heard voices and smelled bacon growing stronger.

The canteen, fixing someone food not that long after midnight, so there was an operation. No German kitchens would have stayed open otherwise. Nor Soviet.

Now, things got delicate. Dare he confirm who was eating? Or simply withdraw?

By now, Sasha would have joined Nikon, and perhaps crossed over to this side of the courtyard.

Too many risks of an alarm if he got close, so Ilya withdrew.

He could always bring back assistance.

But Sasha would need to know.

CHAPTER 23

Vanya let his eyes adjust fully to the darkness as he waited beside an American Jeep parked first in a line with several others in a motor pool. There were also many Two-And-A-Half ton trucks nearby, but the Jeep was the mark of an officer.

Not a staff officer. Those would go around in staff cars, being officious.

A Jeep, on the other hand, was the tool of the lower-ranking officer. The busybody, doing things that saw them directly interacting with enlisted personnel.

In that, it was almost as much a clipboard in his hands as anything.

"Arkadi, you will drive," he murmured to his companions. "Yanina, for now, you will look exactly like a nurse that has been added to the group, and when we take the tank, you will drive while Arkadi and I handle the turret. It will have a co-axial machine gun, so we will be able to engage enemy troops as we move. Assuming it becomes necessary."

Both nodded in the darkness.

It was the height of arrogance, to drive across an enemy base in a stolen Jeep to approach a tank on guard duty. Vanya found himself smiling at what he might accomplish. Everything tonight was fluid, mostly because they had no idea what the Werewolf Legion had planned, but nothing Vanya had seen tonight suggested that they had been wrong to attack.

The Silver Eagle would launch tonight. Or in the morning. Either way, it would have to be stopped.

He checked his watch, noting that midnight had passed. Armies tended to round numbers, so he would presume that a watch had run until midnight, with another team being cycled out at either four or eight in the morning.

It wasn't like duty in a tank that wasn't running would be all that onerous. Prepared for crazy Ukrainian partisans to come over the wire, perhaps, except that who would expect such a silly thing here?

It did make him smile.

"Weapons?" Yanina asked, hefting her Thompson.

"Out of sight," Vanya replied, locating a saddle holster for such on the Jeep and sliding his in.

He still had his pistol. And Arkadi his rifle that went into a matching sleeve. Yanina put hers down flat on her messenger bag with nursing gear in the floorboards in back, then they all went back to hiding, a set of small lumps in the darkness next to the larger ones.

"When do we move?" Arkadi asked quietly.

"When they bring the Silver Eagle outside, as though preparing to launch," Vanya decided. "That will take time and should make sufficient noise. We will simply take advantage of it and pretend to be the team replacing the current group in the tank, taking them prisoner. With luck, nobody will pay any attention."

"And if not?" Yanina asked.

"Then we have a Sherman tank with armor and machine

guns protecting us," Vanya nodded. "And perhaps the need to drive through the fence to escape, while firing backwards into the base to cause trouble for the Legion and provide Sasha and the others with cover."

She nodded.

Vanya had no idea what was going to happen, save that everything pointed to the Werewolf Legion striking tonight. Or first thing in the morning.

If that aircraft took off, New York City might be doomed, so he simply had to stop it.

Idly, he considered what would happen if he parked a tank on the rails and disabled the engine, but that was simply a suicide pact for himself and the others.

He hoped that it wouldn't come to that.

CHAPTER 24

Alois was out of cigarettes.

Cursing, he patted his pockets for more. Finding none, he might have to return to his quarters and get into his foot locker, because he was dead certain that there were none down on the factory floor right now.

Wolf-2 had laid down the law with a bear-like growl, unwilling to allow anyone down there to have cigarettes or lighters, to prevent them from even considering sneaking off to have a smoke.

Not while refueling a rocket plane.

He sighed. Shrugged. Turned towards the door and saw Dr. Gerstenberger seated with one hand up, holding an unopened pack.

"I could kiss you," Alois said.

"I'd rather not," Heinrich grinned. "Sets a bad precedent for the men."

Alois laughed and took the pack from his hand, tapping it down with the reverence of a holy relic before extracting one and lighting it.

The smoke went all the way to his toes, and Alois felt some band of tightness loosen around his chest.

When he had he turned into a worrier?

When he realized that the War was finally—fully—over. That he was allowed one final *Beau Geste*—one grand gesture —by the gods, and tomorrow would have to begin his penance.

"What are you working on?" he asked Gerstenberger as he let the smoke calm him.

"Trying to decide if I should mail a packet with all my calculations to Werner," Heinrich laughed. "I have no doubt that they will immediately bring him to Washington to explain what happened. And I have been listening to you think aloud about the choices we face. The grim duality that the world will fall into."

"Fascism and communism," Alois nodded. "The Americans talk a lovely game of freedom and liberty, but it is all a charade. Their history in Central America gives lie to almost everything they have ever said."

"And they chose to stand up to Stalin in Berlin," Heinrich replied. "I would not have believed that situation would have gone on as long as it did. Or that the Soviets would allow the Americans to resupply the city entirely by air. That they simply gave in astounds me."

"I was amazed that they never moved in and crushed the city with their tanks," Alois agreed. "Never pushed. I wonder if Stalin blinked."

"Someone did," Heinrich said. "What does it mean, though?"

"The Berliners have chosen sides," Alois replied. "Or the Americans finally took their boot off the German throat. And Germany chose the Americans. At least those parts the Russians didn't control. I think Berlin will end up entirely split into two pieces that will never reconcile, because Stalin has memory of twice we invaded them and tried to wipe the Slavs out."

"Königsberg?" Heinrich asked.

"My birth village in Prussia is Poland today," Alois scowled. "Kaliningrad, as those scum call it. Stalin will never let that city go free. So, yes, perhaps von Braun does need your calculations, so that he can build missiles that can reach Moscow from America. And maybe we need to turn ourselves into good, little capitalists, fighting for whatever the Americans call it. As long as we get to kill Russians."

"Chinese?"

"Anywhere those communist scum appear, like cockroaches," Alois nodded. "I expect that Churchill's Iron Curtain becomes a moat, and we will see the rest of our lives watching two giants vie for control, even as all the empires of Africa and Asia disintegrate."

"Do we help?" Heinrich asked.

"Help the communists?" Alois sputtered angrily. "Are you mad?"

"No," Heinrich replied calmly. "Help shatter everything. American. British. French. Chinese. Soviet. Everyone. Inflict maximum chaos and destruction on all players involved, until they have lost so much strength that they all collapse. Let them understand what German and Austria were like in 1946, when people starved to death. Let us bring the entire world to its knees."

Alois was a bit surprised at the vehemence in Heinrich's voice, but only a little. They had met later, after the Pope's ratlines had gotten many of them to safety.

And Alois had done things in those days that he would never share in a confessional booth.

"You have something in mind?" Alois asked, after a moment to catch his breath and ratchet the emotions down a notch.

"Other weapons," Heinrich nodded. "Missions that involve assassinating key players in both imperial service and revolutionary movements. Terrible things like bombing dams and grain silos. Terror, as the point of a spear, if you will. Like you, I have no love of the Americans. Nor that Slavic scum. Perhaps we need to wipe the slate entirely clean and start over?"

"Chemical and biological weapons, Doctor?"

"Whatever it takes, commander," Heinrich nodded.

It sounded like a dangerous escalation, but only in his mind.

Wasn't he about to bomb the Pentagon to strike one final blow for his Fuhrer?

What if he could keep striking?

CHAPTER 25

Sasha had followed Ilya and Nikon to what turned out to be a barracks. Empty, because all the flight crews were in the factory, along with many of the ground teams. Ilya had heard only a handful of men in the canteen, cooking and cleaning.

Empty.

Searching quietly, they had found a locker room filled with what Sasha could only categorize as space suits. Rubberized leather in silver and black, with a variety of straps to tighten things and gloves that twisted into place and latched. Two plugs in the chest he presumed were for oxygen and cool air, as the suits would have to be pressurized and heated to survive at those impossible altitudes.

The headpiece was the most interesting, as it had a helmet that would do a pulp movie justice. A cylinder that bulged in the middle, intended to be lowered over the head and locked into place by screwing it sideways. Generally mirror finished, to the point that he could only barely see his hand inside when it picked it up.

"They will come here?" Lyuba asked, standing beside him and studying the gear as the others kept watch.

"Yes," Sasha said. "But I'm not sure how soon."

"I still lean towards dawn," she replied. "One less thing to worry about when flying, as navigating in the dark at those speeds will be incredibly difficult."

Sasha nodded.

He had a thought so ludicrous that he couldn't imagine that it would work.

"What if we stole the rocket plane?" he asked her.

"How?"

"Capture Fischer and his co-pilot," Sasha said. "Put on their gear and helmets, then get into the plane, did the full preflight, and take off in it."

"This is not that Martin B-10 you stole from Voss last time," Lyuba replied dryly. "This is a rocket-powered sled, driving a rocket plane, with ramjets on the wingtips. Instead of seven hundred kilometers per hour, we would be flying at twenty thousand kph."

"They have not flown the entire assembly," he reminded her. "If they had, we would have heard about it. Instead, there have been glide tests, short flights under rocket power, and acceleration on the rail carrier. Either the system is deeply intuitive, or there is a detailed checklist involved. I'm willing to bet both. Plus, if something does go wrong, Vanya can always destroy the plane with his tank."

"How would we manage it?" she asked.

Sasha took the helmet and rested it on his shoulders.

"How much of my face can you see?" he asked.

"Almost none," she admitted.

"And you are roughly the same size as Ekkehardt Fischer," he continued. "Wolf-3. I can be your radar operator."

"It would be better if you flew and I managed all the rocket systems," she countered.

"If that becomes possible, we will do it," he said. "From the outside, it looks more like a bomber than a fighter, so perhaps we can manage. Is it worth doing?"

"As opposed to?" she asked.

"As opposed to us sneaking back over to the factory, opening a door, and opening fire with everything we have and possibly blowing ourselves up in the process of destroying the Silver Eagle, *Banshee*."

He watched her do the sums in her head. Incredibly risky, yes, but it also let him control the situation. Assuming that the missile actually worked, of course.

They could steal it, fly it someplace safe, and ditch. Probably over the eastern seaboard of the United States, though he would have one hell of a time explaining everything to the Americans.

At least his cover story as an exiled and renegade Soviet pilot would help. Or be utterly put to the test.

Saving New York City from being bombed—again—would absolutely get their attention. And maybe lead to more contracts. Put him and The Red Branch in a position to hunt more war criminals that thought they had escaped justice.

Lyuba watched him.

"Should we simply kill them?" she asked. "Kill all of them?"

"Until they drop bombs on America, everything is purely speculation on our part," he countered. "We've thwarted their crimes, but nobody knows what they intended except us. Plus, we are in Paraguay, and the authorities here are dangerously unstable, given several coup attempts and a short civil war, no doubt caused by American meddling. If we can stop them here, everything continues to remain in the shadows."

"Do we need to come out of those shadows?" she asked.

"You don't think overflying the United States in a rocket plane bomber will go unnoticed?" he grinned.

She shrugged.

"Do you think we could pull it off?" she finally asked.

"I think we can hide in here, waiting for them," Sasha replied. "Capture them. Or have Ilya take them if they stored flight suits in their quarters."

"Send Ilya to check Wolf-3's room," she said sharply.

"Yes," Sasha agreed.

He moved that way, quickly explaining to Ilya and seeing the man off.

"Everyone else, find a place to hide where you can spring out and attack if you have to," Sasha ordered the rest of the team. "We hope they come here, but it might be a time before that happens. Prepare anyways."

Sasha put word to deed and moved to a corner office that was dark, pushing the door mostly shut with Lyuba behind him. He could see out. More importantly, he could hear without being seen. The others vanished.

Now, the wait.

CHAPTER 26

Sasha heard the sound. A door opening. He checked his watch and stirred.

Three eighteen in the morning. He'd been expecting them before now.

An eye to the opening and he saw Ilya approach, then enter when Sasha waved him close.

"They've gone to their rooms to sleep," the man said. "I was in Wolf-2's room with the door cracked to watch. Fischer went into his room, alone, then turned the light off after a few minutes."

Sasha absorbed that and nodded.

Dinner, then a nap before preparation, because the two men didn't have suits in their rooms. A nap made a certain amount of sense, if they'd been up all day and were expecting to fly tomorrow morning. This morning. In a couple of hours.

"Take Oleg and scout the main factory," Sasha replied. "Make sure that they are still fueling the Eagle, then find Vanya and tell him that we intend to steal the bird and fly it away if we can."

Ilya blinked twice, then nodded and fled, grabbing Oleg. That left Nikon here with he and Lyuba.

"Orders, sir?" Nikon asked from where he had emerged.

"Take them both out without killing them," Sasha said. "We'll tie them up and question them, then see if we can pull it off."

"Would it not be better to simply destroy everything, sir?"

"They'll try again, unless we killed everyone involved," Sasha shook his head. "Since they have not yet committed a crime, we become the hunted fugitives at that point. For now, we can embarrass them. That's the best we can do."

Nikon didn't seem convinced, but Sasha wasn't willing to resort to open warfare at this point. They were all fugitives from the Soviet Union. People who had been convicted of treason and purged. Exiled. Unwelcome.

There was nobody that would protect them.

He needed the Americans, as galling as that thought was. The old Sasha, the New Soviet Man, would have rather died, but Colonel Nazarenko had called upon him to stand up for something bigger.

And Peron hated everybody, it seemed, but that one had an Argentine tiger by the tail and simply had to hold on as best he could, every time a new configuration shook the political system like an earthquake.

Nikon withdrew. Sasha closed the door most of the way, leaving the room in darkness. He could smell Lyuba close at hand.

"If we had more time, I'd suggest a proper sendoff," she murmured with a throaty chuckle. "Since we don't know how long, you rest for a time and I'll watch. I still think that you'll end up flying the machine, but we'll deal with that when it comes."

Sasha nodded. He moved away from the door, but Lyuba stepped right into him and he could only move by brushing hard up against the woman. She stole a kiss that got a little involved, but he kept his ears sharp for sound and heard nothing.

Still, a last meal for the condemned, as it were, compressed into a simple kiss. If you could call it simple.

He moved to the desk and rested against it, watching her shadow as the light outside silhouetted her. Strong, dancer's legs. Muscular and sleek. An incredible pilot. And a brilliant aeronautical engineer, on top of everything.

Colonel Nazarenko had truly found a diamond in a coal mine, when he had recruited Lyuba Gradskaya to the Red Branch. In any other circumstances, Sasha would be considering how to woo the woman. How to find a way to make the two of them a team in the marital sense.

Alas, it was not to be. Not today. Not while the Werewolf Legion threatened.

But he would take every stolen kiss he could along the way. Sasha knew that she felt the same way, trapped by circumstances and having to take what they could.

And if they ended up dying doing this, at least he'd known the woman.

But there was so much yet to accomplish, if he wanted to save the world.

CHAPTER 27

Oleg trailed Ilya has they left one end of the building and slipped sideways around the factory.

"If we are seen, you talk," Ilya ordered. "We're airmen from the main base that got drunk, got lost, and wandered over to see what all the fuss was. Clear?"

"Understood," Oleg replied.

He adjusted his walk to add a certain wobble to it. An off-balancing of precise uprightness that would draw the eye away from the fact that his uniform didn't fit all that well. Nor was it decorated properly with rank tabs and unit patches.

A man impersonating.

Oleg had much experience at such things.

He led Ilya laterally, to a blacked out part of the factory that had been silent when they passed earlier. Probably where parts were fabricated, and thus unused at the moment.

The door was not locked, which didn't surprise him. The Werewolf Legion would deal with you if they found you snooping around, so he had to not be found.

Ilya walked beside him on the outside as they crept through darkness. Oleg would confront someone, spewing drunken silliness to distract, assuming that it was only one person and they could be taken down silently.

He had a pistol tucked away if they had to just open fire, thought that would spoil things for the rest of the team.

And Oleg didn't entirely understand why the Major was going to such extremes to protect the Americans, but he owed Sasha everything, so Oleg would protect them, too.

Darkness. Not impenetrable, but deep. Quiet. They moved like hunters, listening to sounds of men calling back and forth in the distance and machines at work.

Oleg found the spot where they had watched earlier. Close to the entrance that would drop them back into the sewers to escape, if necessary. No one had explained what happened after all hell broke loose, but the Major had also made it clear that there would be trouble before this was said and done.

He was prepared.

Oleg crept to the edge of a door and peeked slowly around.

The Silver Eagle, nested on a railcar and ready to take flight. Teams around it at work, all focused inward on the machine with deadly serious intent, rather than the occasional horseplay you got with a group.

But they were playing with rocket fuel here. Dangerous. The smell had a sweet edge that wanted to make his sneeze, but he held still. Any noise would draw an eye, which would immediately turn into a firefight. Several of them, as the others would either have to flee or assist.

Across the way, a man's shadow silhouetted in a second-story window, watching. Presumably the leader of the Werewolf Legion. It was a pity that Arkadi wasn't here to fire a single shot and take the man out.

How much better would the world be with Alois Voss removed? Could the Legion survive?

But the Major had not tasked him with a suicide mission, so Oleg counted noses and status before withdrawing his head and turning to Ilya.

"Vanya next," he whispered.

They backed away and moved deeper into the darkness, Ilya leading.

Circling, they found an entrance and slipped out, moving slowly and deliberately towards the motor pool.

"Vanya," Oleg said quietly. "It's Oleg."

A shadow materialized almost at his feet, knife in one hand.

Arkadi. How did he do that? Except that it was Arkadi, and the man was a miracle worker in his own field. Just as they all were.

They shared a smile, then Arkadi led him around a larger truck into a place of almost complete shadows. The Commissar was there, as was Yanina.

"What news?" Vanya asked as they all knelt in between two vehicles, with Arkadi and Ilya keeping watch.

"Sasha and *Banshee* intend to steal the Silver Eagle and fly it away," Oleg said simply, waiting for the hiss of surprise to die down. "They believe that anything less requires an assault on the base to destroy it and kill everyone. And even that might not be successful."

"And he is correct," Vanya replied, nodding crisply. "Do we hold off on taking the tank?"

"He did not say one way or the other, sir," Oleg said. "I presume that you are a fallback, if something goes wrong and the Legion remains in control of the bird."

"What about the three of you?" Vanya asked. "If Sasha and Lyuba are on the space plane, that leaves you, Ilya, and Nikon exposed to the retributions that might come down."

"Should we attack anyway?" Yanina asked.

"Oh?"

"If they are aboard the plane, their launch will see them off," she nodded. "If the Legion is packed up and ready to leave immediately, do we open fire on the factory and drive them away? Perhaps kill them, but at least damage the facility so badly that they have no choice but to flee?"

"How do we escape later?" Vanya asked her. "The tank will be an obvious target."

"Ilya can lead us," she said. "Or perhaps we hide in the sewer for a day, but simply driving the tank through the wire, then disappearing into the brush ought to be sufficient. Fire draws the Paraguayan military into the situation. An attack will cause all manner of chaos. It is not like we need to fly away here. Simply make it back to our trucks and vanish."

"Ilya, your thoughts?" Vanya asked.

Oleg was impressed. Most officers simply ignored the input of enlisted men and women. Here, the Red Branch was much more egalitarian. Almost more Marxist that the regular military, but that was an improper thought to have.

Accurate, though. And he was no longer a Soviet airman, so perhaps the Red Branch needed to express a higher ideal.

"It can be done, sir," Ilya said. "Arkadi and I should be able to get everyone away. Would it be better if we didn't attack?"

"No, we'll want chaos," Vanya told them. "Fire, explosions, madness run amok. The Werewolf Legion needs to be driven from this facility as if the Americans have arrived to arrest them."

"Sasha spoke of how they had not yet committed crimes, sir," Oleg offered. "That before we stopped them with the wing. And here, they are merely in a conspiracy to do a thing, but if he succeeds, then they fail. And that we risk being seen as criminals to the locals."

"In that, he is correct," Vanya replied. "We stop them, and they are only a little guilty, at least to the locals. If Sasha and Lyuba steal a space plane intending to bomb America, that will change many opinions."

He paused there and Oleg sat on pins and needles waiting as the man thought.

"Ilya, you will get outside the wire as soon as possible and make sure that we are safe to abandon the tank. Work with Arkadi to identify a spot. Oleg, you return to Sasha and update him. You and Nikon might have to escape later under fire, so make sure we know where you will be hiding. I intend to open fire on the factory at some point, either after Sasha takes flight or as we need to rescue him and Lyuba from the wolves. You will use a flashlight to signal the situation when we take the tank so I know which option to proceed with."

Oleg nodded and they spent several minutes working out details. It helped that they had mapped the facility before, so everyone was familiar with locations. And codes.

Now he had to sneak back in and make sure the Major was successful.

CHAPTER 28

Ekke had set a small alarm, just to make sure he didn't oversleep. Not that he had, but it told him to get his ass out of bed and go get ready.

He was only about a third of the way down a long and detailed checklist that they had spent months polishing, but you did those things for a reason. Every time someone had a thought, it got written down and reviewed. Some of them made it onto the list. Others were duplicates or overt paranoia that could generally be discounted.

Like an attack by someone as they finalized for launch, requiring an American Sherman tank to be parked on the far side of the flight line to protect everything.

Crazy, but it made Voss feel better, so Ekke just nodded. His job was to fly the beast, with yet another long checklist of things that would get him to northern Canada and a boat that would pick him up on the morning, running well ahead of the shockwave that would greet an attack on the Pentagon.

And even if they could somehow track him on radar, there was no way in hell they or the Canadians could intercept him. Or even chase him down in less than days or weeks, by which time they would be comfortably south of the equator again and looking for their next job.

Assuming he survived any of a dozen points where the system might fail and explode. They'd tested everything. Run flights in pieces.

Never assembled the whole, let alone launched it.

He was about to make history.

Ekke shrugged everything into place and exited, heading to wake up Lars, but the man was already standing with his door open.

"Ready to go out with a bang?" Ekke chuckled as they headed for the locker room.

"I'm in the rear seat, so I'll go first," Lars countered. "I'll try to make sure that the front of the rocket falls off so you can parachute to safety."

Ekke laughed. How else to approach this topic? Hopefully, any failure would happen so quickly that he was already in hell before the devil knew he'd died.

Otherwise, he was looking forward to seeing the arc of the planet itself from high enough that maybe Dr. Gerstenberger could build them a bigger one and reach orbit someday.

How amazing would it be to sit up on Odin's throne Hlidskjalf and watch the entire world below? And drop bombs on every single Soviet city, before moving on to everyone else?

What would it be like, to be as unto a god?

Such thoughts thrilled him with possibility as he got into the locker room and started unbuttoning his jacket, to change into his flight suit.

Movement caused him to turn to his left.

Sound.

Darkness.

CHAPTER 29

Nikon waited with all the patience the ancient Chinese man had demanded. Unmoving. Shallow, silent breaths to keep himself oxygenated and muscles limber.

Ready to explode into motion once his targets were in place.

Two men. One, a shorter blond, built wiry in the lead. The second, average height and brown hair.

Both shadows moved past his hiding spot and came to rest.

Nikon heard the two open locker doors and stepped to the corner, measuring their locations even as he exploded into motion.

Sasha wanted them alive, unharmed, unconscious. Nikon took a step and struck the taller one across the neck with the blunt shaft of his rochin, a crack that reverberated.

The smaller man started to turn, but Nikon had anticipated him and moved to strike at the base of the ear with a flat stroke. Soft spot, where any number of nerves clustered and were unprotected by bone.

The man went down like a sack of potatoes. Both had. The

Chinese elder had insisted on using the rochin like westerners used fencing sabers. Precise. Elegant. Deadly.

Nikon looked back fondly today on all the hours spent striking targets in training, though he had cursed the man mentally at the time.

But he had learned.

Movement was Sasha and *Banshee* approaching.

Nikon was already down, grabbing hands of the taller German and tying them behind him.

"Oleg, watch the door," Sasha ordered.

Sasha was dealing with the blond just as quickly.

Bound. Gagged. Dragged back into the office.

Nikon returned to the lockers and found the spacesuits. And a checklist that had fallen out of the blond's hands at some point.

Launch preflight. Typed. Front and back of a page.

He went to the office.

"Sir," he said, handing it to Sasha, who quickly scanned it.

"Yes," the commander nodded. "Good. Everything. Nikon, you watch them now. The plans say for both men to get dressed in their pressure suits and attach their helmets and oxygen systems before emerging, to test that they work before launch. We will do that now."

Nikon noted that both men would be out for a time. And groggy. Concussions should be to a minimum, because he had struck soft tissue intentionally.

Somewhere, he remembered that a concussion was sometimes sufficient to permanently ground a military pilot, as nobody could be sure how they would react later to decreased pressures at altitude or to heavy maneuvers.

He supposed that he could have done permanent injury to the men, but the Major wanted them able to answer questions.

And he had heard the conversations about how the Werewolf Legion technically hadn't committed any crimes, though he had missed the aerial battles over Argentina after Pavel had betrayed the team and gotten himself killed.

Good riddance, really. The man had gone foul.

Fortunately, the Major had not held Nikon responsible. Had even gone out of his way to fly training missions with him, instead of shipping him off to Ireland to wait for a replacement pilot to be found.

Assuming one was.

For that alone, he owed the man. And would do this with precision.

Nikon checked respiration. Both strong. Both men would recover.

Why the Major wanted them alive and healthy was not his concern.

His responsibility was to do his job better than anyone else could.

There was a war in the shadows.

CHAPTER 30

Sasha stripped off his various layers and got down to his shorts. Beside him, Lyuba did the same, distracting in spite of merely changing clothes.

Comparing them in his mind, she was almost exactly Wolf-3's size. Roughly one hundred and seventy centimeters tall, and around sixty-eight kilograms. The suit went on like it had been tailored for her.

His suit was a bit tighter, but had been made with space, once he adjusted a few straps.

Checking the list Fischer had carried, he located the brief-case-like device in the locker and pulled it out. Two flexible tubes with air-tight plugs marked for oxygen and cooling. Insightfully, the two were different sizes, so there was no question which was which.

Smart. He wondered if the Nazi program had originally come up with that idea, or one of the Werewolves. He attached both lines and turned the machine on, then moved on to the next item and attached his helmet.

Air he could breathe. Cool air blowing around his body.

The checklist said to proceed to the launch point now.

Sasha quickly scanned the rest of the checklist and noted that German precision had verged onto didactic, but this was the one time when that worked in his favor. Even the note that they would plug in to a radio system on the Silver Eagle and test things before launching.

Sasha cut the air lines and removed his helmet. Harder than it looked, but possible. It took Lyuba a moment to catch on, then she did the same.

He waved her close and moved to the office.

Both Nazis were still unconscious. The temptation to simply end them was great, but Sasha did not wish to turn into that sort of a man, so he simply nodded.

"I believe that we have what we need," he told Nikon. "Leave them gagged and come."

The man followed them to where Oleg kept watch.

"You two wait here, then slip out and move on to your next responsibilities," he ordered. "We will walk into a lion's den and attempt to get out alive. Oleg, you will warn the others if something goes wrong. Nikon, you update Vanya and his team so they are ready to move as well. Timing will be important, as we may need the tank to rescue us. Or avenge us if the worst happens. Are you men ready?"

Both nodded, so Sasha turned his systems back on and attached the helmet that would hopefully keep him alive when they got to the top of the atmosphere.

Lyuba grabbed his hand and squeezed it once, for luck he presumed, then Sasha opened the door.

Pausing, he remembered that he was Weber the radarman here, so he gestured her to lead, as she was pretending to be Wolf-3.

And then then went out into the hallway, found the door, and emerged into night.

PART THREE

EAGLE'S FLIGHT

Lyuba tried to walk like a man. Straight spine. Slight hunch forward she remembered from a few shorter men trying to look like bulldogs.

The life support system in her hand was a weight, but the notes said that it would attach to the system on the ship and be shut down until the end of the flight. Later, it would be attached to their parachute harness and turned on again, so they could bail out of the space plane at high altitude and not die of exposure before landing.

Wherever they were going.

Sasha had handed her the checklist. It went into a pocket across her stomach like a kangaroo's for now, and she walked like a man with a purpose. A mission.

A terrorist attack intended to weaken the United States and perhaps draw them into a war in South America, at a time when the Communists were on the verge of capturing China and Europe was being divided into two ideological components.

She found that she missed being a loyal Soviet scientist/pilot, but the job required a different expression of her patriotism. As Sasha had put it, they were trying to stop all wars from breaking out. Or at least escalating.

Buying time for everyone to recover from the terrible experiences of the war. The Americans had turned on Stalin. The British had tried to remain friendly for a time, but the Berlin Blockade was probably a breaking point that would be generations healing.

Her job, then, to keep the Nazis from scoring even a single late goal, however little it might matter beyond simply showing that they had not surrendered on the pitch, regardless of what had happened in and above Berlin.

Like rabid dogs, some people could not be dealt with. Hopefully, Sasha would see that and they could wipe out the Werewolf Legion once and for all.

Even the Americans would not be able to overlook something like this.

She entered the factory and walked down a well-lit corridor, isolated by the sound of the fans in her ears and her breath speeding up as things got extremely dangerous.

Oleg would follow. Ilya was supposedly somewhere in this darkness, watching and ready. If all went well, he would join Vanya and they would take over the tank at the same time that the railcar was being rolled out into the open for the first and only flight.

Men turned as she emerged. The suit had no audio pickups on the outside, so she could watch them applauding her, but not hear anything inside her helmet.

The silence was eerie, but calmed her. It was like turning off the motor on her old canvas and wood Polikarpov Po-2 biplane and listening to the wind whistle and whisper over the wings as she glided in to bomb frantic and terrified Germans below.

Not these men. These had been the ones above in Messer-schmitts and Focke-Wulfs, risking stalling at low altitude to try and shoot her and her sisters down. Many had tried. Only a few had ever succeeded.

Tonight, she might offer her sisters some level of payback for the risks they had taken, where any failure of their aircraft stranded them deep behind enemy lines, a place where being executed was the **least** of their worries.

Rabid dogs.

She walked.

One giant of a man emerged from the crowd and held out a hand to shake.

Sigmar Schmidt. Wolf-2. Voss's second in command, but perhaps only a coin toss had put him in ahead of Ekkehardt Fischer. Or recruiting sequence, as both were the inner circle of the Werewolf Legion.

She shook his hand firmly. Fischer would have.

He turned and led them to the Silver Eagle. Squared off edges almost hex-like, up close. Both wings almost the same size and shape. Front and rear seating, so she would be flying, because there was no way to put Sasha up front.

At least she was already used to doing crazy things in the air.

At the top of the ladder, she turned and saw Alois Voss, watching from above in his office. Next to him, the infamous Heinrich Gerstenberger who was the cause of so much of their troubles.

Mad scientist, indeed.

Both snapped to and gave her a Nazi salute, one arm rigid. Around her, Lyuba saw the others do the same.

It felt utterly icky, but it was necessary, so she saluted Voss the same way. Then turned and repeated it to the Legion. Sasha did the same.

And it did make her feel better. It reminded her that there was evil in the world yet. That for all the war criminals they had hunted, or might yet hunt, the ideology itself had not been wiped out.

These men were proof.

And she was about to steal their space plane.

Smiling inside her helmet, she climbed in and settled, locating the spot to lock in her air breather, then attach it to the onboard systems.

Behind her, Sasha boarded, then Wolf-2 closed them up.

It had begun.

CHAPTER 32

Alois lowered his hand and dug out a cigarette. It was acceptable that he'd smoked half of Gerstenberger's spare pack already. He would likely finish it by the time the Silver Eagle launched.

Then they could load up into the caravan of vehicles and head to Sao Paulo for their ship.

At that point, the Werewolf Legion would vanish entirely for a time. And hopefully some fool would sell Johannesburg as a destination to whatever spies or gestapo came to inquire. He had no intention of getting anywhere near South Africa today. At least not yet. There were other places in Africa he might try, but French Indochina looked to be a good place to drop rocks on fragile buildings.

Or bombs.

"It begins, Doctor," he said, turning to Heinrich.

"We are a little early," the man replied. "Should we start loading up the last of the gear anyway? There is little most of us can do at this point, once the Eagle is fueled. One team to push it into position, then off on our destiny, eh?"

Alois considered it. They had walked through the entire

process as a dress rehearsal, minus only the fuel, so there should be no surprises at this point. And everyone had a copy of the checklist that had caused him so much heartburn creating.

"Yes, I think that would be good," Alois decided. "You take Wolf-5 and that group and start loading the men who will be traveling with us. The others can remain behind, as if we were merely going out to see how the aircraft worked and will be back in a few days. None of them need to know any better."

"I shall see to it," Heinrich nodded, turning and exiting with his usual flourish.

Alois turned back to his window and lit another cigarette, knowing that he had to stop when he stepped outside this room.

But by then, all would be in motion.

For once, he let himself smile.

CHAPTER 33

Sigmar watched Wolf-4 slowly drive the little rail engine up to the rear of the Silver Eagle, almost delicately connecting. Men swarmed, connecting lines and confirming that there were no leaks anywhere before giving the thumbs up.

"Testing radio," he said simply, checking the list.

Ekke always got dour and serious at moments like this. Curt, verging on rude, so Sigmar was not surprised to hear Lars reply.

"*Sehr gut*," the man said on the scratchy radio.

They hadn't bothered with anything sophisticated there. Mass was the enemy at a time like this, so just enough to talk on the ground lines while they were connected. Once aloft, the Silver Eagle was on its own.

And Ekke would be in his own head now. It happened. But it was also why Alois had chosen him to fly the vengeance weapon. This was that moment when everything would need the sort of utter precision that Ekke brought to his flying.

Any one mistake and they would be tumbling out of the sky. Or simply exploding as a pretty fireball visible for kilometers.

Sigmar turned to Wolf-4. Ulrich waved his readiness..

"Silver Eagle, let me know when you are ready," Sigmar said.

Silence. It was a long list, and they needed to complete several steps inside the cockpit before the railcar was pushed out into the open.

Outside, it would be close to dawn. Perhaps verging, but they only needed to be certain that the sun was up when the bird overflew Washington D.C. an hour after launch. Because the Americans would never see this coming. Literally.

He could not wait.

CHAPTER 34

Sasha would be handling communications. There was no way to make Lyuba sound like a man, so he hoped that he could keep things short and blunt and that would be enough. Until they got outside, he had nowhere to run.

Instead, he had a copy of the checklist that had been left on the console. German thinking. Trebly redundant in all things.

Outside, the slightest jar as the pusher came up behind them and connected. Sighs as airbrakes connected and they were almost ready to go.

He switched to the intercom so he could talk to Lyuba without being overheard.

They should have been swapped, mostly because she was better at the technical things that Weber would be doing from back here. Sasha wasn't sure he was a better pilot than *Banshee*, though.

"Checklist to section five complete," he told her.

After all, the Germans had a plan in place. He could follow it, at least to the point where someone bombed an American city. He would skip that part. And hopefully they would be able to ditch the space plane safely. He would like to survive this escalation.

"Section five complete," she replied evenly. "Ready to deploy."

Sasha nodded and switched back to the outside line.

"Ready to deploy," he said quietly, using a deep voice that would hopefully carry, but not be identifiable.

"Silver Eagle, stand by to deploy," a man's voice said. Presumably Wolf-2, but Sasha had never heard him speak.

Today, everything needed to be precise, professional, and short.

No mistakes, from now until they reached New York City, except that flipping to the back of the checklist, Voss had decided to strike the Pentagon in Washington D.C. instead, with maps and aerial photos handy to make a final approach, including altitude and timing, because the bombs would have to fall a considerable distance on a radio-controlled glide path.

There was even a version of the American bombsight that had been so secret, where you put in your speed and altitude and let the machine run down to the actual bombing.

Not that he needed it, but Voss had taken every detail into account.

Pity it would fail.

Outside, a slight lurch as the pusher engine got them into motion.

They were committed.

CHAPTER 35

Oleg watched the combined vehicle begin its slow progress out on the curved rails that would line it up. No alarms, so the Major and *Banshee* had gotten aboard and were prepared to steal the machine, as astonishing an outcome as that could be.

He moved to the exit and started when a shadow moved.

"Oleg, it's Nikon."

And it was, though Oleg had not understood how well that man could sneak. Oleg had been a fast-talker when trouble broke out. Usually, it had been sufficient with sergeants. Not so much with commissars.

They made their way to the motor pool and located Vanya and the others.

"Look sharp," Vanya said as they got close. "We are not anyone they will recognize, so I intend to bluff these men into simply getting in the jeep when we arrive, then leaving. There is potential for sudden violence, but Ilya is outside ready for us and Sasha will be in a position to launch when it happens. Timing will be critical. Oleg, you drive. Your role is a corporal of the secret police who does not understand why he had to get out of bed so early and will make faces at his officer's back. Clear?"

Oleg couldn't help but to smile. He almost saluted the man unconsciously, because Vanya, like Sasha, understood how Oleg operated, and was willing to take advantage of those strengths.

It would be an easy role. Simply pretend that Vanya was any of the **other** commissars Oleg had known in his time. Men and women with little imagination and a terrible addiction to the precision of regulations, regardless of the actual situation.

He moved to the driver's seat as Nikon and Arkadi rode in back with Yanina. It was a bit crowded, but Oleg supposed that the commissar had brought a team to handle the tank itself and a nurse in case something went wrong. And even sergeants in South American militaries would automatically default to an officer who brought his force of will to the situation.

And, if all else failed, they had guns and a few grenades that could be shoved inside the tank to kill the crew, if all hell broke loose out there.

They were settled. And armed. And ready.

"Drive," Vanya ordered.

CHAPTER 36

Vanya set his mind to a social superiority that was hammered into commissars when they were chosen. Men and women willing to enforce a *proper revolutionary mindset,* often on poor peasants only barely off the farm and completely lost in a modern army.

The war had been hell, wiping out a significant portion of two generations in the process of stopping the Nazi beasts from overrunning the world.

Tonight, they were trying again, and he would not allow it.

A hand found his pistol and touched it once for luck, but he would rely on Nikon and Oleg—and Yanina—opening fire if it came to that.

He had to run the most colossal bluff he could remember.

They circled along the outside of the fence, well away from the factory and those rails. As they passed the barracks, he could see two trucks backed up and men moving about. Loading for their escape, no doubt.

Hopefully, in the chaos, they would simply chose to flee entirely rather than remain in place and fight, because he did not have the manpower to stand them off. The tank would give him the edge he needed, but Vanya had to take it away from whoever had it, and that would be the critical point.

If the men inside were part of the Werewolf Legion, it would probably come to a fight. If they were simple Paraguayan airmen from the other base, he could likely bull them into submission for long enough.

He didn't need much time. Sasha and Lyuba in the air, then his team running like hell, possibly shooting, because Oleg and Ilya had both confirmed that there was a factory for making rocket fuel in there somewhere.

One spark, and the building might detonate. The Legion would have other problems to face than chasing him into the brush.

The airstrip was lit, but there were no planes. None on this side at all, which did not surprise him, but was good nonetheless, because they could not strafe him as he fled, either. It would require the Legion convince the colonel in charge of the other side to launch his own aircraft, and that would take time.

"Oleg, park where that one light tower is exactly behind us," Vanya ordered. "I want that light in their face as we talk."

On the rail, a small engine slowly pushed the car that held Sasha and Lyuba around a circular curve until they were pointed due north, with that hill at the end that had been added in order to skijump the space plane at the last minute.

They were moving at a snail's pace, so it would be a few minutes for everything to settle there. Then, presumably, the engine would detach and withdraw to safety inside the building, along with everyone else, leaving him in command of the field.

For what it was worth.

Vanya ignored the space plane. Instead, he concentrated on the tank. Everything hinged on his being able to remove the crew inside without a battle.

Oleg drove like a chauffeur, which was surprising, but the man was an actor and Vanya had given him a role to play. All of them had roles, but Oleg thrived in that place.

Good to remember.

The Jeep slowed, then stopped. Oleg cut the engine. Vanya could hear the crews working to get the space plane ready, but only because the train engine made noise and the rest of the night had fallen to a pregnant pause, poised with anticipation.

The hatches were all open. That was good. The night was warm, and the crews appeared relaxed.

A man emerged from the commander's hatch and studied him as Vanya stepped out of the vehicle.

"Who is in command here?" he asked crisply in Spanish with an upper class accent he had picked up in Argentina.

South America was an extreme case of classist society, frequently with racial overtones measuring in fine gradations how much Spanish blood one had, compared to native.

The man in the hatch perked up and stood a bit taller.

"I am, sir," he said warily.

"Clear your men from the tank," Vanya said peremptorily.

"Sir?"

"Out," Vanya snapped angrily. "Now!"

Other heads popped up, wary and confused.

Vanya took a step.

"We are from the Interior Ministry in Asuncion," he said with a chilled malevolence. "You have been relieved. Return immediately to your barracks and speak of this to no one. Am I clear?"

Flinches. In Latin American countries, the Interior Ministry often fulfilled the same role as the Ministry of State Security—MGB—did in the Soviet Union. Secret Police, separate from the Army and entirely antagonistic.

The *Midnight Knock* that left empty apartments behind, often as much a terror weapon as law enforcement action.

The words were like a magical incantation. Bodies came flying out of the tank rapidly, forming up in enough of a line for his purposes.

Vanya's crew had exited the Jeep already, standing on the opposite side where the bright lights on the tower would blind them to faces.

Vanya relied on the tone of his voice, and many years as a commissar and officer. And he was facing a group of men perhaps grown slack enough to warrant a dressing down in the process, but that would take time he didn't have.

Five men, seemingly shivering in spite of the warm night.

"Get in the Jeep and drive away," Vanya scowled. "Speak to no one. The Interior Ministry will supervise the launch, and determine what happens next. We will be watching you, as well."

He left it cryptic. In a situation like this, less detail was better, because he could already see the men glancing at one another and trying to fill in details. Having none, someone would invent some. Those would be passed along to others as fact, regardless of his orders.

No, actually, because of them, which would be even better.

The sergeant scrambled to the Jeep. Others piled in and one of them got it started, grinding the gears badly in his haste to depart.

Vanya rotated like a gun turret on a battleship to watch them go, then finally allowed himself a smile.

"Mount up," he said simply, then found himself last as the others went like mountain goats up the green cliff-face of a Sherman tank.

Vanya found himself commanding the battle field.

For what it was worth.

CHAPTER 37

Ilya sighed and flipped the safety back on his Thompson. The range would be too great for any sort of accuracy, but he could have at least distracted by opening fire on the tank over here if it had come to that, a tongue of flame in the darkness that would have piled all manner of confusion onto the situation.

The Commissar had the tank. Assuming it was armed, he had an impregnable fortress. Sasha and *Banshee* were almost in place at the south end of the railway track. Ilya had found the original game trail that they had taken to get here, along with a few others that would possibly get them back to their trucks even faster, though he might ignore them for ground he knew anyway.

So many things could go wrong yet, but they had made a start.

Shortly, the aircraft would launch. Then Ilya needed to be prepared for whatever happened now that Vanya had a tank that could resist just about anything anyone could do to stop it, short of bringing in another tank.

Ilya hadn't seen anything in the motor pool other than a set of old British armored cars, a handful of Daimler Dingo scouts and one Daimler Armoured Car with the quaint, little 2-pounder main gun that could not threaten a Sherman. Useful as crowd control or resisting a small rebellion, but not effective on any real battlefield.

It was a pity that they couldn't steal anything more interesting, but they had no cargo aircraft capable of carrying even something as small as a Dingo.

At least not today. Perhaps he would talk with Sasha about ways to improve their field equipment, if the Red Branch ended up running more commando operations.

Who knew what the future would bring?

For now, he settled in and watched as the rocket train got ready to make history.

CHAPTER 38

Lyuba had gone through the entire checklist once, just to familiarize herself with it. A second time as they worked each step with metronomic precision. If nothing else, the Legion had set out a very effective battle plan that covered many contingencies, including acquiring and installing two ejector seats that would rocket both her and Sasha clear of the aircraft at the same time, presumably to safety since they would have air and parachutes.

Behind her, the train had disconnected, leaving them alone on the rail as the engine quickly withdrew. According to the checklist, Wolf-2 would indicate when they were ready to fire all of their rockets, a series of switches that she could reach with her left hand without moving her arm.

They would be accelerating at several G's and she would be pressed deeply into her seat as they built up speed.

"Disconnecting railcar locks," she said into the intercom, working her way ever down the list.

"Confirm disconnect," Sasha replied.

The Silver Eagle had been held in place with one pin to keep it stable. Now, it was resting in a cradle like a pair of fingers ready to snap an atlatl forward. They would reach maximum speed on the ground and hit the ramp, at which point she would pull back on the flight stick and they would be airborne.

Then she would ignite the ramjets and the craft would soar.

Or explode.

She confirmed the fuel indicators as full, though they would empty almost fast enough to watch. Controls were stable. Everything was ready.

It was her that was having second thoughts, but they were far past the point where they could back out of this mission.

Was she about to kill herself and Sasha on this mad quest? Even flying as a Night Witch paled to a space plane, but it had to be done. The Werewolf Legion had to be stopped, and this was the only way to ensure that they didn't just do it again somewhere else. Somewhere like Iraq or maybe the vast wastes of Saudi Arabia, where they could work in secrecy and strike Moscow with surprise.

No, once they told the Americans about this attack and the Flying Wing, Lyuba was confident that that those men would proscribe the Werewolf Legion. Perhaps Sasha could even convince the Americans to hire them to hunt the Legion.

Was there a better revenge, considering how many Nazis the Americans had hired to keep them out of Soviet hands? There might even be a few opportunities for accidents to happen to a few of the most terrible ones that had escaped justice.

She could hope.

For now, she looked out the thick canopy glass as a lone figure walked across the runway towards her. Wolf-2. Sigmar Schmidt.

He came to rest on her forward left flank and waved one

hand over his head. The signal that all of his people had gotten to safety.

On her other side, she had watched Vanya somehow charm or threaten the crew of the tank into taking the Jeep and leaving in a mad hurry, so she could only assume that they were ready.

Was she ready?

Lyuba crushed her doubts and waved back to the Nazi, then watched him walk away.

"I show ready to launch," Sasha said on the intercom when the last Nazi vanished inside the building.

Not quite as good a flying partner as Yanina, but she'd keep him.

Where she was going, Lyuba Gradskaya would need all the friends she could find.

CHAPTER 39

Alois was standing next to the trucks, loading up the last of their trunks of gear when a man came barreling out of the barracks.

"Commander! Commander! Come quick!"

Gerhardt Richter—Wolf-8—was close, so Alois nodded for him to accompany. Wolf-7—Tilman Koch—would supervise. They walked in the direction.

"Sir, something happened to Wolf-3," the man said.

"WHAT?"

"We found him in the locker rooms, sir," the man—the cook—said. "This way."

Alois began jogging, goading the man to run to keep up. A hand confirmed his Walther on one hip.

In and through, they got to the locker rooms where Gerstenberger had stored the flight suits and gear for the Silver Eagle's crew. The man led him to a back office, where a medic was working on Ekke and Lars, both a little groggy.

"Someone heard a noise, commander," the cook said. "When we investigated, we found them tied up and gagged, stuffed back in this office."

Alois ignored the man and knelt next to the medic.

"Status?" he demanded.

"Perhaps a mild concussion, but nothing severe," the medic replied. "Both men were struck blows on the neck designed to stun and render someone quickly unconscious. The common term is being sapped."

"Ekke?" he asked his best pilot.

Ekke blinked and started to rise, but the medic pushed him flat again.

"I need to take you to the infirmary," the medic said. "Both of you. Observation to make sure you weren't hurt worse than it appears at first."

"Rest, Ekke," Alois ordered.

"Alois," Gerhardt leaned down to murmur in his ear. "If Ekke and Lars are here, who is flying the plane?"

Alois shot bolt upright, eyes bright and wide with surprise.

"We must stop them," he said. "Whoever it was will discover how slowly and painfully someone can actually die."

He took two steps, then the building began to rattle. A roar like Joshua's horn filled the night.

The Silver Eagle had just launched. There was nothing he could do to stop it.

Then the sound of gunfire and explosions filled the night.

Alois started to run.

CHAPTER 40

Lyuba crushed her doubts and reread the final command in Section Nine.

She was ready. Sasha was ready. Vanya appeared ready.

The Silver Eagle was ready.

"Stand by to launch," she said, striving to keep her tone professional and crisp.

History. And possibly death.

"Standing by," Sasha replied.

Section Ten.

Right hand on flight stick. Left hand opened the covers on the fuel pumps and set them to pressurizing. A moment later, ignition occurred, programmed directly into the pumps and not requiring any human intervention, save to make adjustments on flow as needed.

The railcar was designed to simply run as fast as it possibly could, in order to fling its payload into the air with the highest possible speed.

The rockets behind her lit and began to push as well.

Outside, the night had grown bright as day with the several tongues of flame pushing her north at a slow and steady acceleration. The ramjets would come when they got airborne and not before, because of how poorly they performed at slower speeds.

No, theirs was the thrust to shove her into the sky.

Even as smooth as the rails were, the bumps were transmitted up her spine and into Lyuba's skull, like a mad woodpecker tapping.

Sounds intruded, somewhere behind her, but she remained solely focused on the hill ahead, racing ever faster towards her as the speeds increased.

Relentless.

Exhausting.

Impossible.

"All engines firing normally!" Sasha called over the dragon's roar that accompanied them.

Lyuba would have nodded, but her head was pressed back against the rest, leaving her hands and feet free and not much else.

On her console, a row of green lights reinforced his opinion. They were committed, a cattle in the chute. As long as everything remained green, it was as good as it would get.

The sled hit the bottom of the ramp and her stomach dropped as they suddenly began to climb. Even as smooth and slight as the initial incline was, it was like those roller coasters she had seen in films.

Their acceleration was above three G's and still rising. It wasn't difficult to breathe, but it took muscles and concentration. She appreciated how much higher the oxygen saturation in her suit was right now to help. Not pure, but enough her her shallowness of breath.

There was a marker sign, located halfway up the hillslope, lit by a pair of bulbs, one on each side. The sled reached that point and Lyuba pulled back on the stick, pretending that the vehicle was a glider rather than her Polikarpov biplane that had been as nimble as a bumblebee.

Everything here had to be smooth and precise.

The Silver Eagle took flight.

CHAPTER 41

Vanya had known to avert his eyes from the terrible illumination that filled the night. The sound was so monstrous it was as though the world was ending, a roar somewhere between an angry dragon and a giant tearing a piece of cloth larger than Ukraine.

He had the commander's spot in the tank, with the turret still facing the outer wire. Below him, Yanina was ready to drive, with Oleg and Nikon manning the main gun and coaxial machine gun next to it. Arkadi stood next to Vanya up top, with his rifle out of sight, but ready to bring it up and practice his marksmanship. Vanya would rely on the big American .50 caliber machine gun.

He felt the engines start, but the sound was lost in the noise. Yanina, right on time.

Vanya triggered the mechanism to spin the turret, bringing the main gun to bear on the north end of the factory. All of the work and lights they had seen at been at the south end, with the north itself dark, so he presumed that to be the machine shop.

The tank lurched into motion, turning quickly and heading north some. Not far. Merely enough that anyone who might have thought to line up an anti-tank cannon or rocket would miss if they fired right now.

"Gunner, stand by!" he yelled over the noise, finally receding as the rocket plane moved away from them in a haze of smoke that would also help.

Vanya didn't need to hit another moving vehicle tonight. Merely a barn.

A hand on his foot was the signal that they were ready to fire.

"FIRE!" Vanya yelled, closing his eyes just in time for another burst of light and flame as the long barrel spoke.

Any other time, and that heavier 76mm long-barreled cannon would sound authoritative. Tonight, it was an angry squirrel, chittering his pique in a nearby tree.

The building did not resist, though. Brick over a metal frame, the shot punched right through with a spark, followed by a polite detonation inside.

"AGAIN!" He ordered.

The cannon spoke, rocking the tank sideways like a rowboat hitting a larger ship's wake. This second shot hit something important. Or the first shot had broken something and allowed a spark to find a fuel source.

The top of the building came off as it exploded, filling the night with flames. More flames blasted open doors and shattered windows. The shockwave rattled the tank even worse than the cannon firing, to the point that Vanya dropped down inside, thought he didn't bother to pull the hatch closed. He couldn't see as well, but there would probably be people opening fire soon anyway.

Best to be behind armor.

Yanina drove a line as straight and true as the rails. In the distance, he could hear the changing sound that he hoped indicated the space plane lifting off. It was growing quieter, if nothing else.

Oleg had been firing the main gun. He had the co-axial going now, with Nikon reloading. A Soviet tank would have a machine gun to the rear, for being encircled, but the Americans only added one on the bow, pointed away from everything while they fled the scene of their crime.

The noise was more compressed inside, so Vanya waited a bit, then opened the top hatch again and peeked just enough for a clear view. Arkadi had ducked as well, but popped back up and was scanning the horizon, though he had not fired.

The factory was burning. Uncontrollably, if the height of the flames reaching the heavens was any indication. And the secondary and tertiary explosions he heard, presumably as barrels of things got hot enough to detonate.

Chaos.

Good enough. Better, nobody appeared to be fighting back, but Sasha had chosen a night when the Werewolf Legion had appeared to be packed and ready to leave, which might mean that most of their small arms were in storage or already departed.

After all, they'd had the Paraguayan military send a tank and crew as base security tonight.

"Yanina, make for the wire," he ordered, still watching backwards.

Then he thought about what was coming and nodded to Arkadi, both of them dropping inside and closing the hatches overhead. Arkadi made his way to the forward machine-gunner spot, probably to get out of the way in the small confines of the vehicle.

Across the way, lights were starting to come on in the Paraguayan side of the base. Presumably, fire-fighting teams would be rousted and sent.

Vanya wondered if they'd managed to disable such teams inside the Legion factory, or if those men had already gone to work inside and he was in a bad place to see them.

Conversely, those men would be safe from being shot, as long as they generally stayed away from walls on this side.

"Oleg, cease fire," Vanya ordered. "Keep watch and be ready to kill anything with the main gun, but let them get distracted by the fire for now."

Oleg nodded and went back to the gunsight, watching. Yanina turned on one set of tracks, skidding some because she hadn't bothered to slow down, and then was racing directly at the cyclone fence topped by razor wire that marked the boundary of the base.

The tank tore through it by driving over one of the posts and snapping it off with a slight jolt inside. Outside, there had been a strip kept cleared, but hardly more than ten meters wide in some places, and mostly brush beyond, slowly turning into trees.

He let Yanina drive. And she proved to be as expert as everyone else at their tasks.

"How far in?" she yelled.

"Out of sight and under any trees you can locate quickly," Vanya said. "We are not staying long with the beast. Ilya will find us, then he and Arkadi will get us home."

Or at least back to the trucks, hopefully not molested by anyone where they had been left several hours ago.

Or he would steal something else, like they had the tank.

He had enough guns. And killers willing to use them. Even a small revolutionary bandit group would think twice about bothering him in the brush.

Outside, more dull, quiet explosions marked the end of the Werewolf Legion base.

CHAPTER 42

Sasha concentrated on the controls. The backseat was for a flight engineer, as much as anything, with so many systems that needed to be watched.

Thankfully, Lars Weber had marked a few with colored tabs, indicating safe margins, even as he had left a list of things to watch and a timing to every event.

Sasha had thought that they were going fast when they lifted off. Then the ramjets had ignited and slammed him back into the seat again.

Everything was green. Remained green. Fuel tank indicator spiraling down almost as fast as the speed and altitude indicators spiraled up.

The original design for the Silver Eagle from before the war had suggested that it would climb to an altitude as high as one hundred and forty-five kilometers, at which point, the craft would be traveling at more than twenty thousand kilometers per hour.

If they weren't about to go as high or as fast this morning, it was still mind-boggling, watching the temperature gauges measure their heat of passage. Hot enough to fry eggs on the skin.

Outside, they had already flown higher than Sasha had ever gone in any aircraft. The morning sky was darkening again as they climbed above most of the atmosphere. Craning his head over to look down, the ground raced by, Paraguay already giving way to the immense green depths of Brazil's Amazonian reaches.

The original flight path had them heading west-northwest, around 343 degrees true and a surface distance of roughly seventy-four hundred kilometers.

It pained him that such a craft wasn't being used to deliver people between the two continents, though he understood that today's propeller-driven civilian airliners would eventually give way to jets with the range and speed.

Too much technology was dedicated to warfare. To killing people. And he was willing to admit that there were people out there that needed to be killed. Executed like mad dogs for crimes against humanity. The Americans had rescued many German scientists and carried them off to hidden laboratories. The Soviets were no better, he knew, having worked with a few such men that had been taken to the East to serve their punishment.

Too many more had still gotten away with the help of the Pope and his bishops, but that man had a deep and abiding hatred of all things communist. Probably because Marx and Lenin were far closer to their Christ than he and this catamites would ever be, in their silk robes and gold-trimmed temples.

Sasha would not allow the Werewolf Legion to bomb Washington, DC. Or New York City. London. Paris. Berlin. Moscow.

They must be stopped, and the Silver Eagle represented the single greatest threat that he had to confront.

So far, he reminded himself. He and Lyuba still had to make it someplace safe, then bail out, land, and presumably be arrested by American authorities who would put his new identity as a purged exile to the ultimate test.

Could he convince the Americans? Or was he doing all this, merely to end up rotting in another prison somewhere, unwelcome by any side? Or at least until the Soviet Union requested that he be sent back. Not even Gennadi would be able to rescue him then, Sasha expected.

He shrugged, as much as he was able to under the pressure.

"Fuel countdown," Sasha announced. "Engines shutting down in roughly ten seconds."

"Confirmed impending shutdown," Lyuba replied over the intercom.

He could hear the tenseness in her voice. She would have been better in this seat than him, but Sasha still wasn't sure if he'd have been a better choice in front, as she had flown the plane like this was her fiftieth mission instead of her first.

Outside, the ramjets continued to howl, a *Banshee*-like scream that he felt in his bones and counterpointed the deeper roar of the massive rocket motors behind him.

Rather than let the tanks be pumped dry, the plan called for the ramjets to be shut down manually once fuel fell below a certain level. That kept one from continuing to fire for a second if the other ran dry faster, possibly inducing a destructive yaw into their flight at the time when margins were microscopic.

The rockets would drink it all up anyway.

The *Banshee*s ceased their wailing.

"Jettisoning ramjets," Sasha announced.

Up front, Lyuba would be concentrating on flying smooth.

He flipped the cover, then the trigger. Both housings popped free and immediately vanished, to fall to earth somewhere below.

If anything, the aircraft felt lighter. Smoother. More graceful without those beasts on the wingtips. Certainly, he relaxed a notch.

Only one notch, though, because they still had perhaps ten more seconds of thrust from the rockets before the aircraft truly became a glider.

Next stop, America.

CHAPTER 43

Alois was knocked on his ass by the shockwave. That probably saved his life, because the building began spewing rocks and shards of metal at him.

He'd made it outside the barracks. Dawn had risen and filled the space with warm light though there was a chill in the air.

Then shit began falling, so he grabbed Gerhardt and pulled the man towards him as he scrambled under the truck that had been waiting nearby.

Around him, a stone rainfall fell.

"Get under cover, you fools!" Alois yelled at the others.

Men began heeding his advice, ducking behind the truck or back inside the barracks.

"What is happening?" Gerhardt asked.

"Somebody stole my plane," Alois growled. "Everything after that is a distraction intended to keep us from doing anything about it."

He controlled his temper, then nodded to Wolf-8.

"Get to the local side of the base," he ordered. "Roust their fire brigades, though I doubt that anything is salvageable from the factory. We'll still need to keep the fire from spreading."

Outside, the initial avalanche of stones had ceased, though Alois could still hear smaller explosions inside the place.

All that fuel. All those volatile chemicals, however carefully stored, it would do them no good when there was a fire.

Gerhardt moved. Alois emerged and located several of his men, all ducked down and a little white-faced.

About where he would be if he didn't know the truth.

Then the sound of machine guns. Heavier ones than the Sturmgewehr 44 his men carried, so possibly that tank the locals had assigned. Why was it firing? Who was it firing at?

"Orders, sir?" Wolf-7 asked.

The trucks were backed up to the loading dock at the south end of the factory, where it seemed that the north end was burning. He didn't have much time.

"Locate Gerstenberger and get him into a car and away from here immediately," Alois said. "Ekke and Lars are in the barracks getting medical treatment. Grab them and the doctor treating them and take the whole group to town. Do no wait for the rest of us."

"On it," and Wolf-7 started to jog.

Wolf-5—Friedrich Becker—was supervising. Alois grabbed him.

"Take what you can get in the next five minutes, then move the trucks outside the gates and wait for me," Alois ordered. "Leave the gates open for fire brigades and anyone else. Wolf-8 is summoning the Paraguayans to take charge of this situation. They're merely getting it a day earlier than planned. Make sure you have all flight crews accounted for. Tilman will have Gerstenberger in his charge. I'm going to find Wolf-2."

The man merely nodded and went back to supervising the

local crews. Not having brought his aircraft, Alois had left his mechanics and ground crews behind, where they had already made their way to Asuncion to meet up with the rest of the Legion.

Alois began to jog around the south end of the building to locate the rest of his Legion.

Hopefully, those fools had the sense to get out of a burning house.

CHAPTER 44

Vanya had the Fifty Cal pointed at the sound, but it turned out to be Ilya emerging from the brush. Probably intentionally making noise so people knew he was there.

"Status?" Vanya asked.

"Complete chaos," Ilya nodded. "Nobody has emerged to chase you, but that is only a matter of time, since tank treads leave such an obvious trail."

Vanya smiled. If there had been any way to drive the tank to the trucks, he might have considered it, damning the consequences to get out of the area quickly. As it was, he expected roadblocks would go up quickly headed south, but they had already made plans to flee north to the town of Pozo Colorado, which let them wait for a time, or quickly race east and cross into Brazil.

As far as he knew, nobody had seen anything, and if they had, his people had all been wearing Paraguayan military uniforms that looked to be American surplus. They had stripped them off and left them in the tank, so he faced the morning in blue.

Vanya counted noses and had everyone.

"We depart here and get to where we can go to ground," he reminded everyone. "Ilya, you and Arkadi are in charge until we get to the trucks."

Vanya grabbed his messenger bag and climbed down as the others got organized. Everyone was in the blue of the Red Branch again, so they would be obviously something military and important if stopped. It wasn't to be helped.

Worse, he was in command of the Red Branch until he could talk to Sasha or Gennadi for more orders, so they had to follow the plan as Sasha had laid it out originally.

Get out of sight. Hide for several days until they knew what had happened. Then, and only then, figure out if they needed to flee Paraguay. And to where.

The aircraft were with Yuri, back in Ireland, where they would hopefully be safe, as long as nobody was captured.

It was fortunate that none of his people had been hurt, as a hospital trip right now might tip their hands and end with all of them arrested as terrorists.

Not that it would be a wrong assumption, but he'd rather escape and wait to hear back from Sasha.

The space plane had lifted off. He had watched it vanish into the morning sky with his own eyes, and not seen any explosion, so he held in his heart that they were safe.

As safe as they could be.

"Moving out," Arkadi announced, breaking his reverie. "Everyone remain as quiet as possible and remember to drink water. The walk is about four kilometers, then we have a long drive ahead of us."

Long, yes. Not as long as Sasha and *Banshee's*.

Lyuba let the aircraft talk to her.

The space plane, as they were going to the edge of space. She had heard suggestions that it might be measured at fifty British miles altitude. Or one hundred kilometers. It had never mattered before today.

Still, some incredible number that felt like it would be better suited to a book.

But she was here. Flying it. Outside, the only sound the dying whistle of air on the hull, as the rockets had gone dry and left everything to inertia.

"Autopilot set to three-four-three true," she said calmly. "Sasha, how close to Washington do you wish to go before we do anything?"

At these speeds, there would not be long to act. Especially not as wide as this craft would take any turn she chose to initiate.

"Bear another five or ten degrees to port as you can," Sasha replied. "We will use Florida's Atlantic coast as a mark to get us over inland South Carolina. Near Atlanta, Georgia, which is a major city we should be able to see from up here, we will bank back to starboard sharply, stabilize, and then eject, presumably somewhere over North Carolina or Virginia. That aims the plane well out to sea when it comes down, so nobody will be at risk beneath it, and lets us land safely."

"To be immediately arrested?" she asked, already starting to lean into the sluggish controls.

Sluggish, only in that the atmosphere at this altitude was so thin that the wings had little to lift against. Below, in the early morning light, the Caribbean Sea raced by, with the islands of Hispaniola and Cuba ahead.

"At first, we will be merely rescued, if I understand Americans correctly," Sasha replied. "Later, we will have to contact the authorities, who may indeed take us into custody. It is not to be helped."

"No," Lyuba agreed. "The alternative was another war. And the Werewolf Legion winning this round."

"They must not win any rounds," Sasha replied darkly. "I fear that the Red Branch may have to go on without us, if the wrong decisions are made, but at least Vanya can get everyone else home safely and contact Gennadi."

Lyuba kept her commentary to herself. Vanya was an exceptional officer. And pilot. But he would never replace Sasha. Without their commander, she expected that the Red Branch would simply be quietly closed down. Presumably, everyone else repatriated back to the Soviet Union and quietly awarded medals for what they had managed to accomplish thus far.

Saving America twice, even as paranoid as Stalin and his flunkies had gotten, should be important. Nobody won at that point, if another war broke out. Especially as the Americans were the only nation with an atomic bomb.

They might choose to annihilate Moscow if it came to that.

Perhaps the rest of the world, as well.

Outside, the nose of her space plane had come around some. She could just make out the tip of Florida in the distance as she made delicate adjustments to bring the nose down.

The original plan called for much longer at the peak, but that assumed a landing at the far end Hudson Bay or one of the islands that marked its mouth.

Again, safely crashed and away from prying eyes that might steal the design and replicate it. Presumably, to bomb Moscow or Leningrad in turn.

Some weapons were too evil to exist. Especially if it was an American one carrying an atomic bomb.

Nobody in the world would be safe.

"Florida in sight and flight path adjusted," Lyuba called. "I estimate that we will be flying roughly fifty kilometers off their eastern coast. Descending from maximum elevation."

"When you reach land, be prepared to come about to zero-six-zero true," Sasha replied. "That should keep the plane on a path roughly parallel to the northeastern coast as it flies over the Atlantic and crashes. Hopefully, somewhere where it cannot be recovered later."

She nodded and concentrated on her flying. Outside, the air had begun to thicken. They had peaked at fifty-two kilometers. Some one hundred and sixty thousand feet as the American's might measure it.

Airspeed was still excessive, but the design was intended to bleed speed into heat as it reached the thicker air. Lyuba was not intending to skim and bounce back into the sky, as the original Silver Eagle Amerikabomber plan had foreseen. Gliding like a rock skimming across calm water, from Europe to New York City to somewhere on the far edge of the Pacific, where the Imperial Japanese Navy would have picked up the survivors.

The whistle of air on the hull was a faint background noise, but she knew that it would get louder. Insulated by her helmet, it would probably be something she felt in her sternum more than anything, and that was fine.

The sky ahead was so utterly perfect that Lyuba felt like she could see forever.

Now she just had to make it there.

CHAPTER 46

Alois located Sigmar inside the factory, guiding a team with fire hoses to try to do something about the raging blast of heat that was destroying the place.

And all the evidence, so he was less angry about that, given a few minutes to think.

He walked close and tapped a shoulder.

"Leave it," Alois ordered. "Let the Paraguayans fight this. We must depart immediately."

Sigmar turned an angry growl at him, then swallowed on recognition.

He shut the hose down and dropped it at his feet, motioning the others across the way to do the same. Two hoses weren't going to do anything at this point, anyway.

"Evacuate!" Alois ordered at the top of his lungs, waving the men angrily away.

Nobody had any air gear, and the smoke was getting thick, in spite of blue skies he could see where there had been a roof an hour ago.

Alois would have thought a badly-timed accidental fire, but

he knew better. Someone was covering their tracks, having stolen his plane.

Who, he had no idea. Nor did it matter at this instant.

They had to flee immediately.

Outside, the air was calm. Cool, but warming quickly.

Alois counted noses and had all of his men, both flight crews and mechanics, accounted for.

"Everyone out the gates," he ordered. "*SCHNELL!*"

They began to move. Alois set a hard jog of a pace, forcing them to keep up. Better if he pushed right now.

He'd already been pushing his luck, but someone had decided to push back.

How long did he have before someone arrived to arrest him? To arrest all of them?

Alois didn't think that it was Paraguayan Interior Ministry, though their rivalry with the military was deep and well-known. The military was entirely on his side, seeing the rocket as a way to get even with all their neighbors for territory stripped off in the war with Argentina, Bolivia, and Brazil nearly a century ago, offset some by victory in the Chaco War fifteen years ago.

Paraguay had a deep and abiding—and well-earned—distrust of their various neighbors. And several recent civil wars and ongoing turmoil inside as well.

That had been his logic behind using it as a base. People who would support him for their own reasons, and people he could blame things on later.

Until someone stole his eagle.

The group fell into their normal workout lines, pilots on his left and radarmen on his right in two columns behind him. Alois set a punishing pace when they fell in, so the gates were reached quickly. Already, the first fire brigade trucks were winding up sirens and closing, so he made his way to the right and let them pass.

Ambulances for his men were unnecessary, as everyone appeared to be unharmed. Those dealing with chemical fires behind him would need the assistance.

Outside the gates, the two trucks were parked. The staff car he would have ridden in with Heinrich was gone, which was good. Ekke and Lars and a medic as well, so he would catch up with them at the hotel already reserved for the Legion under the authority of the Army.

He would be armed when he walked in, in case it was another ambush.

They came to rest by the side of the road. Alois gathered all his men and confirmed that only insiders were with him today. Cooks and others could help the army, or stay out of the way, but they did not belong to the Werewolf Legion.

Nor had he met any worth recruiting among the many that had cycled through.

"We have been betrayed," he told his wolves in a dark, somber voice, drawing a growl from them. "Someone attacked Ekke and Lars in the barracks. They stole their suits, and boarded the Silver Eagle. I do not know who it was, but I will find out."

"Attacked?" Sigmar snarled quietly, but that was Wolf-2, and Ekke was his best friend in the world.

"Injured, but not bad," Alois nodded. "I have sent them ahead with Gerstenberger and the medic."

"Then who was flying?" Ulrich—Wolf-4—asked.

"I do not know," Alois replied. "Someone who believed that they could manage the Silver Eagle. And did, since it took off cleanly and got out of sight. It was not Wolf-3 aboard. Do we know what caused the explosion?"

"The tank opened fire on the factory building, commander," Kurt Schulz said loudly. Wolf-5's radarman.

"WHAT?"

"Two rounds from the main gun, covered by the sound of the rocket engines," he nodded. "At the north end, followed by raking fire from the machine gun. They immediately fled over the wire at that point, and we were too busy trying to control the fire. Plus, all of our weapons had been packed and transported to the hotel ahead of us."

Shit. The man was right. Alois had his Walther. And that might be the only gun available, unless he broke into the base's armory for more. Was it worth it? Or did he slip in while they were concentrating on the fire?

He looked around and located Jusep, standing by the door where he'd be driving the lead vehicle.

"Guns?" he asked the sergeant.

Not a team sergeant. That had been his rank in the army. The man was a bodyguard when Alois needed him. And a killer.

"Four, commander." He nodded to the front of the truck.

"Good enough," Alois said. "We must be prepared for the Paraguayan Interior Ministry to intercept us, so we'll put one each front and back of both trucks."

He turned and located Schulz again.

"You said they went over the wire?" Alois asked.

"Took out a post, then drove up the berm and into the brush without any more shots, sir," Schulz nodded.

Not the Ministry, then. They wouldn't have destroyed everything, either, but would have just swooped in and arrested everyone. Wouldn't they?

Of course, given Paraguayan politics, even worse then

Argentine, anything was possible. Or Brazil, Bolivia, or Argentina had chosen to get involved.

And stolen his Silver Eagle, damn them to all hells.

Alois took a deep breath and focused.

"Assume trouble," he told his men simply. "We will outrun it to Asuncion, if we can, then immediately depart, rather than spend the night as intended. I wish our foes to be chasing us all the way to the coast, rather than able to somehow box us in. At the hotel, rearm yourselves, then sleep with a pistol under your pillows until we sail away. Mount up."

He moved to the front truck and took the passenger seat. Sigmar would ride in the second, with the men in the beds under the canvas tarps.

"Roadblocks?" Jusep asked as he got the beast into gear and started down the road to the highway.

"We will negotiate them if we can," Alois replied. "And blast through them if we cannot. I have no wish to spend any time in a South American prison, Jusep."

The man nodded. None of them did. Too easy for their pasts to catch up with them, if they ever came under official observation.

Everything until now had been done in the shadows.

And into those shadows he would need to vanish quickly.

CHAPTER 47

Sasha watched his controls, but with the rockets shut down and the ramjets ejected, the Silver Eagle was a high-altitude glider at this point, and Lyuba seemed to have everything under control.

Skin temperature outside hot enough still to cook, but that was speed turning into friction as they got lower. Still impossibly high compared to any aircraft he had ever flown in. Still several times the speed of sound, but that number was also dropping steadily.

Eventually, they would be low enough to safely bail out, but that was not yet, and they did not have that long at these speeds.

"Landfall!" Lyuba called as they entered the mainland of the United States. Sasha had known many Americans during the war. People who ferried into Persia the planes that he took onward to the Soviet Air Forces fighting the fascists.

Generally friendly, and he had not chosen them as his enemy. Nor had he chosen to become an exile from his homeland. Worse, when news got out of what he'd done here, and the Flying Wing, how badly would his reputation be tarnished, to the point that he might never be welcomed home?

It had been necessary to stop another war. And to establish the Red Branch as a mercenary company that was not tied to the Soviet Union, in spite of the air crews all being Soviet. Ex-Soviet. Or at least Ukrainian for most of them, though most Westerners would not understand that distinction. Some of his countrymen had joined the Nazis to try to throw of the yoke of Lenin and Stalin, but he had not.

Kyiv was still a far older center of learning and civilization than those Mongol-descended barbarian punks in Moscow. Or the Georgian.

But he might never go home. It was time to make peace with that, and hope that Gennadi's cover as the owner of the factory producing Nightviper aircraft could withstand American inspection.

Else they were all doomed.

"How close is Atlanta?" he asked her, stirring from his introspections.

"Already visible in the distance," she replied.

"Come even and begin your turn," he ordered. "Use that to bleed velocity, then prepare to eject shortly after that."

"Understood."

Shortly, he would land on American soil. Hopefully, they would not take it personally.

Lyuba watched the temperature gauges showing how hot the skin was outside. She had no idea what alloys had been used, but they had withheld everything so far.

She was about to test them.

"Initiating turn to zero-six-zero true," she called, fighting to bank around to just past northeast.

The plane buffeted under her hands, but that was expected. The controls were mushy but growing more stable as things bit the wind and turned it to her control.

Height: twenty kilometers and falling steadily. A little over sixty thousand feet.

Speed: Mach 3 and falling quickly as the plane turned its belly into the windstream.

She had to fight the tendency of the nose to rise, gliding edges designed to eke out the most distance possible in free flight.

Normally useful, but she could smell the end of that invisible runway in front of her, when they would cross back out over the ocean, never to be seen again because she could not cross to France or Portugal at this point.

They were committed.

At least the Nazis had installed ejection seats. And automated them to the point that either passenger could trigger them, sending both into the sky.

They were an arrow, falling out of the sky. Slowing, but not enough that she could actually consider landing this beast. Nor, from what Sasha had told her, did she want to, given that war criminals like von Braun would immediately understand what had been done.

And how to add atomic weaponry to it.

No.

"Time to departure?" she asked Sasha, leaning into the pitiful air brakes and asking them to do something, anything to buy her more time.

"At most, thirty seconds," he replied. "Turning on my portable air system now."

Lyuba located the switches to cycle over to the machine that was attached to her parachute, and brought them live again. Then checked all the settings.

There was no air up here. None worth breathing.

They would have to fall a considerable distance, but the system was designed to be overridden, so that the parachute didn't open immediately on deployment.

Sound German machining and thinking, that perhaps Wolf-3 and his radarman might have to eject at these tremendous heights and speeds, and need to get down to the thicker air before they deployed.

"Stand by for ejection," she said, leveling the aircraft out perfectly flat and setting the autopilot to keep the nose down. Not much, but enough.

Full air brakes deployed. They wouldn't last long under the pressure, but she didn't need them to.

Her steed had carried her as far as it could, and there had been no easy and safe way to dispose of the two bombs underneath, so the whole was going to be destroyed at sea.

"Standing by," Sasha replied.

She took a moment to study the landscape. Low mountains covered with forest. Coastline ahead, coming up quickly.

Lyuba reached down and located the handle for the ejector, popping out the pin holding it in place, then jerking it upwards hard.

The thing came off in her hand.

Overhead, explosive charges blasted the canopy upwards, where it immediately vanished from sight, letting the thickening air come in.

Then the rocket under her seat ignited and thrust her up into the windstream.

She had a moment to watch her Silver Eagle continue on straight and true, then she began to fall.

PART FOUR
AMERICA

Sasha knew he would be bruised and battered from the ejection. It still beat dying at sea, so he gritted his teeth as they slowed so hard, then began to plummet.

They had to fall a considerable distance to get to where they could safely ride the rest of the way down. The automated altimeters had both been set to five thousand feet. Higher than strictly normal, but he preferred having those extra seconds to deploy the emergency backup if something did go wrong.

Both he and Lyuba were experienced at this sort of thing, though ejection seats were a wonderful new invention he highly approved of. Test pilots often had moments when the plane suffered some dramatic or traumatic failure in the air.

That was what test piloting was for, to find all those strange corners where the math and engineering were blind. Especially as nobody really understood jet flying and had only recently broken the sound barrier.

Every year, someone came out with a new aircraft that was a step better than the one before, although his test flights in early MiG-15 aircraft had convinced him that the Soviet Air

Forces had been absolutely correct to move that one to mass production.

It was a fantastic flyer. At some point, it would prove a wonderful surprise for someone, though he had no doubts that the American and British would be hard at work, coming up with their own counters.

Or, at least, the American would. The British appeared to be on the verge of general bankruptcy as their Empire melted away everywhere.

How many years would they try to hold on as a First Rank power?

Knowing the British, long enough to destroy themselves. They had lost most of Ireland. India was gone. Australia and Canada were growing more and more independent by the day.

Perhaps the sun would set, but the Americans were already racing to fill in the gap. Berlin was just the next step after the Monroe Doctrine.

Below, a sea of green, broken by roads and rivers. Up country, as the Appalachian mountains started to his northwest, but Lyuba had gotten them pointed closer to the coast. He thought that they would come down more in southern Virginia, but that was merely a guess at this point.

He had maps. And emergency supplies that would see them safe for a few days, if they had to hike.

Sasha let his fingertips spin himself slowly around until he located Lyuba, a little above him and more or less ahead, since he could see sunlight glinting off the tail of the Silver Eagle as it raced out of sight.

She appeared to be watching him, so Sasha tucked his legs under him and sped up. Proof that he was awake and in control. A moment later, he flattened everything back out and watched her do the same.

Good. Both had made it clear. Both were awake and in control, with their air systems running.

He could only imagine how quickly one of them would have died, exposed to the cold, thin nothingness of the upper atmosphere, but the suits were insulated, pressurized, and safe.

Quality work, even if the men who had done it were servants of evil itself.

Now, he had to make it safely to the ground.

And turn himself in to the American government.

CHAPTER 50

Lyuba delighted in the free-fall. She had never jumped from anywhere close to this height. Paratroopers routinely went from under two thousand meters, and they had been closer to twenty thousand, so it felt like forever.

At least the suit worked. And the altimeter would trigger when she got to the thicker air below.

Green seas of leaves beckoned her. Low mountains on the northwest. Ocean to her right and ahead, where the Eagle had already vanished from sight.

Hopefully, from history, too.

The air was thickening around her, but the helmet insulated her against the whistles, leaving only spiderwebs tugging at her hands and feet.

Sasha was falling close enough to track him. And awake, which was good. The sky was bright and she worked to keep the sun more or less behind her, so that she could track the north and east as she fell.

Somewhere down there were cities. Towns. Roads.

America.

She had never been. Never been interested. Her war, unlike

Sasha's, had been on the front lines in her biplane. And she knew that Sasha held certain regrets that he had not spent as much time flying in combat, but Gennadi had quietly explained to her that Sasha's willingness to obey orders and go where he was needed most had actually factored in more than one might expect.

A man who would do the right thing, regardless of personal cost.

A lesson she was working to take to heart, though nobody could ever accuse a Night Witch of cowardice.

As they fell, Lyuba could make out a road, running perhaps one-ten true, with a river in the distance and a town she could see from the grid of roads and houses. They would not land very close to it, but she could aim for the road itself, then hopefully someone would pick them up and carry them the rest of the way.

Their silver spacesuits and blue uniforms would certainly get someone's attention.

Freefall. Thickening air. Rising sun. Land rushing up to meet her.

Then her chute deployed, jarring her. Looking around, Sasha's had deployed as well, and they were falling more slowly now. Very little control, and she wondered if it was possible to make adjustments to the round design of a parachute to allow someone to control it.

Possibly a glider design of some sort? More rectangular than round?

She filed that thought for later, and concentrated on where they would land. Trees. A pair of lakes that she hoped to avoid, though the suit came with a small inflatable emergency raft because the original plan had involved possibly landing in Hudson Bay itself while the boat raced to get them.

The one road continued to approach, and Lyuba willed herself to somehow guide the winds that got them there. Better than hanging up a tree and having to climb it down.

Never a good thing. Too easy to risk a broken leg.

Then they were falling towards an open field. Possibly graveled over, like one might store large vehicles, but a godsend for someone with no control over their descent.

Lyuba concentrated on her fall and roll, going back to all the lessons on how to escape a plane that had decided to die mid-flight.

Impact, collapse, tumble, safe.

Grab the cords and draw them tight, though there was hardly any breeze this morning. Get the parachute under control and wadded into a ball, tied off with the cords she disconnected.

Automatic.

In the distance, Sasha had just missed landing in a tree, and was doing the same, so Lyuba began walking his direction, parachute under one arm and air-system in hand.

They met in the middle and she put things down to remove her helmet and shake out her hair from the quick tail she had tied it into earlier.

A man emerged from a building at the edge of the road, dressed like a farmer in rough clothing and pulling a flat cap on.

Sasha had removed his helmet as well, and put it at his feet, holding down the wad of nylon as he disconnected hoses and put the air system down. That sounded good, so she did the same as the stranger walked slowly closer.

The man stopped some twenty meters away.

"Mornin'," the man called in an uncertain voice. "Everything okay here?"

"We're fine, sir," Sasha called back, not moving any closer as the stranger looked quite skittish. "Could you contact the authorities and have them send someone over? I have a most amazing story to tell and it cannot wait."

Lyuba nodded.

An understatement, if anything.

CHAPTER 51

Sasha was riding in a Ford pickup, next to the open passenger window with Lyuba between him and John, the man who had owned the land where they had arrived in America. John was in the process of driving them into Danville, Virginia, the town he had seen from above as they fell.

If he remembered the map, they were not far from North Carolina. Perhaps four hundred kilometers to Washington, with Richmond roughly midway between.

"A rocket plane?" John asked. "Like in the movies?"

His accent was hard to follow, but it took Sasha back to the war. To other friendly Americans he had met.

"That's right," Sasha replied.

"Where is it now?" John asked.

Lyuba was remaining generally silent, so he had to carry the conversation.

"Hopefully, crashed in the Atlantic," Sasha told him. "The men we stole it from were intending to bomb the Pentagon in Washington. That's why we had to act when we did. There wasn't even time to call in the authorities."

He didn't bother mentioning that the Paraguayan Army—

at a minimum—had to have known something of what was going on, though he doubted that the top leaders were aware. They might have objected to possibly taking center stage in an American invasion intent on retribution.

"Well, I'll be damned," John said. "But you folks saved the world?"

A bit more extreme than Sasha would have said it, but in the end, not necessarily wrong.

"Something like that," Lyuba offered quietly.

"And you, little lady, you flew that thing?"

"That's right," she said. "Sasha and I have both been professional test pilots before this. And both flew combat aircraft in the war."

"You?"

Sasha listened as Lyuba gave the man an abbreviated and somewhat sanitized history of the 588th Night Bomber Regiment and 46th Guards Night Bomber Aviation Regiment.

The Night Witches.

John whistled when she finished, but Sasha could detect a new respect. Americans were very paternalistic, feeling that women were too fragile for combat.

It was a stupid idea, but he had long since given up trying to get so-called more-advanced societies to see how they treated their women and minorities.

Nobody ever listened.

Then they were in Danville, running down quiet streets lined with brick buildings and many trees.

John turned at an intersection and they were in a quieter-yet area.

"You two have been up all night and not eaten, right?" he asked.

"That's correct," Sasha agreed carefully.

"Then let's get you to the diner and get some grub in you," the man said. "I'll have Gayle call the sheriff and he can come listen to what you've told me."

Sasha nodded when Lyuba glanced up at him.

They both had American dollars in their emergency packs. Plus the suits they had stashed under the seat had contained packs with more Canadian and American dollars as well.

He wasn't rich, but he supposed that he had far more money on his person than might be safe.

He also had his Shanxi pistol packed, as did Lyuba.

John had whistled at the uniforms and heard their initial explanation of the Red Branch. The cover story version. That had been what convinced the man to drive them to town, where he had grown progressively more friendly over the last hour.

They pulled into a parking spot in front of a diner. Wide glass windows. Well lit inside. White and black tiles and walls.

People. Americans.

Sasha exited the pickup and Lyuba followed. They trailed John into the place, watching heads come around and conversations stop as folks saw their uniforms. And, possibly, firearms.

He wasn't sure what the modern American rules were, as most of the rest of the world only saw westerns.

A woman approached, a little wary.

"Three, Gayle," John announced. "Breakfast, then I need you to call the sheriff's office and have them send someone around, because my new friends here have one hell of a tale to tell."

Still wary, the woman grabbed menus and led them to a booth, somewhat away from more farmers at the counter.

"Coffee?" she asked.

"Yes," he and Lyuba replied, then she left them all alone.

He had eaten with Americans at those bases in Persia. Here, he was simply astounded at the options available. Even better than Argentina, at least when not eating with the General at his palace.

Lots of choices. And seemingly endless supplies of food, from what he had seen, just walking through the diner.

Sasha had been born in Imperial Russia in 1913, just before the Great War with Imperial Germany. Before the first revolution. Or the second. The Western Powers Invasion. The Bolsheviks. Stalin.

Then the Nazis.

His entire life had been one of deprivation and warfare, but that described all of Ukraine. All of the Soviet Union. Much of the world.

America had suffered no war. No hunger.

And he had time for at least one American meal as a free man, before the government arrived, so he would enjoy it.

Whatever came after.

CHAPTER 52

Sasha watched the policemen enter.

One big man, with a star on his collar. Not Yuri's size, but not much smaller. The second was thinner. Shorter. Younger.

Both locked on him as they entered, then blanched when they saw Lyuba next to him. She had let her hair down, collar-length blonde locks that framed a heart-shaped face and brilliant blue eyes.

At the time, he hadn't understood her motives. Now they were perfectly obvious.

Both officers reset from whatever gruff intent they had brought with them and relaxed.

Sasha had just finished a T-bone steak and two eggs over easy. Hash browns. Several cups of coffee he had diluted with cream and sugar for no other reason than they were free on the table for anyone to use.

Lyuba hadn't consumed as much, but she was a smaller woman. Not small. Not light. A compact gymnast with the brain of an engineer and the face of a fashion model.

John looked up at Sasha's face, then looked over his shoulder.

"Bill, good, join us," John called, waving the two men closer.

Bill nodded to his deputy and that one moved instead to the counter. Not that Sasha was entirely surprised.

Complicated situation. And it would only get worse.

Sheriff Bill slid in next to John across the booth from Sasha.

"Bill, this is Sasha Kryvenko and Lyuba Gradskaya," John introduced them, impressing Sasha immensely because he got both names right, having only heard them a few times when they first met. "Folks, this is Sheriff William Rogers. He's in charge around here."

Sasha nodded and held out a hand for the man to shake. Rough skin. Not a man who lived in an office pushing papers around. Lyuba surprised Bill by also shaking.

Bill turned to John.

"Gayle passed along a note that you had some sort of situation here," Bill said simply.

"Watched these two fall out of the sky in space suits this morning, Bill," John nodded intently.

"Got those in my truck. They got a story about a bunch of bandits down in Paraguay that you need to hear. Then probably get on the horn to Richmond or Washington and get someone down here to hear it as well."

Bill turned back to face Sasha, eyes boring in.

"Kryvenko?" he asked simply.

Sasha turned to show him the Red Branch patch on his shoulder. Lyuba did the same.

"I am the commander of an international mercenary aviation company called the Red Branch," he began. "We operate out of Ireland, but have been working jobs in South America most recently."

Gayle brought Bill a mug of coffee as Sasha explained—in very thin details—who they were and how they had ended up in a diner in Virginia, while those folks who had finished their breakfasts found reasons to stay around and listen. Many goggled in surprise.

At one point, a midde-aged man entered, found a booth nearby, and started writing in a notebook in such a way that suggested a reporter.

Possibly a man about to break the biggest story of his career. Assuming that Washington didn't lean on him to keep it off the wires.

Back home, a Commissar would simply say no and that would be the end of things. Unless you felt like landing in a Siberian labor camp.

Bill studied him—them—when Sasha finished and started adding things to a refilled coffee mug.

"That's it?" Bill asked, somewhere between incredulous and irritated.

"No, sir," Sasha shook his head. "That only covers the basic details. Those things that I expect the American government won't classify as Top Secret when they get involved."

"And you insist that they do?" Bill pressed. "You could have had John drop you at the bus station. Caught a ride to Richmond or Baltimore, then a boat back to Ireland. Or South America. Nobody needed to know."

"The American government needs to know," Lyuba spoke sharply. "This is twice the Werewolf Legion has tried to attack you. Twice we've stopped them, and we were almost too late this time. Something needs to be done."

The anger in her voice was all the more impressive for how controlled it was. John and Bill both still flinched in the face of her ire.

Bill studied her for a moment, then turned back to Sasha.

"Might take some time to arrange," he said simply.

Sasha reached into his pocket and pulled out a ten dollar bill, placing it on the edge of the table, where it would more than cover the three meals and coffee. And have some left over for Gayle.

Wasn't his money. Was, in fact, Voss's, which made it all the better to spend in a diner in Virginia.

"We have cash, if someone could get us a hotel room," Sasha replied. "We can stay there. Walk around town and perhaps shop or at least sight-see, while you contact the necessary people and get them here. My team in Paraguay should be safe, though I expect that the Werewolf Legion has probably escaped by now. They'll need to be found. Hunted down. Something."

John nodded. Bill seemed less convinced, but nodded after a moment.

"Y'all need to wash up?" John asked.

Sasha looked at Bill.

"Let's get them down to the station first," Bill decided.

Sasha nodded and slid out of the booth.

It had begun, whatever this next phase was going to bring.

Welcome to America.

CHAPTER 53

Lyuba had answered questions, using her beauty and charm to distract the poor policeman who wasn't certain how a woman could be a pilot, combat veteran, and aeronautical engineer.

American women were housewives or secretaries. Not soldiers.

Still, she and Sasha got processed quickly enough. And walked across the street from the police station to a nice enough hotel. They were not far from downtown, with shops running down both sides of the street and regular traffic, both vehicular as well as on foot.

They had gotten checked in. Settled. Bored, so she had knocked on Sasha's door, and now they were walking.

Mid-afternoon, but she was still too wound up to consider sleeping, in spite of being up for thirty-six hours at this point.

Lyuba knew that she would crash at some point. Not yet.

Their uniforms caused heads to turn. And the babushkas had already begun gossiping, because she watched heads come together and secrets get murmured back and forth as they walked from shop to shop.

For a tiny town or exceptionally large village, it felt as

wealthy as Moscow. Stores filled with all manner of goods. Pricey, but they had dollars to buy a few things. And Sasha had shared how much he enjoyed letting the Werewolf Legion pay for things from the stash of bills in the their emergency gear.

Mid-afternoon. Ice cream parlour. Warm summer day. Lyuba could not resist.

The number of options inside astounded her. Almost frightened her. She ended up with blackberry ice cream in a cone. Sasha got chocolate.

They found a shaded bench outside, on the edge of a park, and enjoyed themselves, as locals walked by, some nodding politely and others staring.

The pistol on her hip might have concerned them. Lyuba really didn't care.

A man appeared out of the traffic. She recognized him from the diner this morning, where he had sat and taken notes. Sasha had suspected him of being a newspaper reporter.

Brown suit. Nice hat. Blue tie.

Tall and lean. Distinctly American in the way he walked and stood.

He came to rest in front of Sasha and stood politely.

The ice cream wasn't quite gone, but she hurried to crunch that last bite and savor it.

Sasha did the same.

The man waited.

Finally, he took that last step.

"Addison Walker," he held out a hand to Sasha. "Danville Beacon newspaper."

Sasha rose to greet him. Lyuba did the same.

"Aleksandr Kryvenko," Sasha introduced himself. "My associate, Lyuba Gradskaya. We are of the Red Branch."

"I heard part of your story in the diner this morning,"

Walker nodded. "But only part. How much would you be willing to fill in at the start, and then which details might you be willing to share about this Silver Eagle? I gather some sort of rocket?"

"An antipodal aircraft, Mr. Walker," Sasha replied. "Lyuba can provide you much better details on the craft itself, but we could talk."

"There is a restaurant nearby," Walker offered, gesturing to his right. "Perhaps some coffee? Then maybe an early dinner, depending on how things go?"

"You do understand that the government might clamp down on all of this when they hear, yes?" Lyuba asked. "Prevent you from publishing anything?"

"This is America," Walker smiled. "They can get me in trouble *after* I publish it, but the law prevents prior restraint. It might be worth the consequences."

She shrugged. Sounded like an insane way to run a society, but she was an outsider here. Even Sasha had at least known many Americans during the war.

She had lived in Ukraine, Russia, Ireland, Argentina, and, she supposed, Paraguay, at least for a few weeks.

Mostly Russia and Argentina most recently. Neither of which were well-run, either.

"Do we have a deal?" Walker asked.

She turned to Sasha. He commanded the Red Branch, at the end of the day. Even Gennadi—who was Colonel Nazarenko in mufti—was only a tangential presence. For now.

"I will repeat to you what I told Sheriff Rogers," Sasha offered.

"Thank you," Walker replied. "I missed some details there. More importantly, though, I want to get your story, Sasha. And yours, Miss Gradskaya. I would like to hear about the Red

Branch. What it intends and how it came to be. The government might classify everything about the Silver Eagle, yes, but I cannot imagine that they would quash tales of heroic deeds and fantastic pilots saving the world, no?"

Lyuba managed to not roll her eyes at the man, but it was a close thing. None of them had set out to be heroes, though she understood that Gennadi had practically demanded it of Sasha.

Their job was to hunt down those Nazi war criminals that had not been captured by the Red Army or rescued by the Americans. Men like von Braun or Dornberger, who should have both been hung exceptionally slowly to draw out their execution for what they had done during the war. The slaves they had murdered in their mad quest to conquer the world.

Those two were probably beyond her reach, protected by the American government instead of facing a judgment at Nuremberg. There might be others. Certainly Achterberg had only gotten away from them for a time.

And now he was in hell where he belonged.

Walker turned and held out an elbow to her, like, she supposed, a Western gentleman might find appropriate. Because he didn't understand a New Soviet Woman.

None of them would.

Perhaps she needed to do something about that, too.

CHAPTER 54

Sasha was already awake when the knock came at the door. They had bought some clothing yesterday, and sent their uniforms to be quickly cleaned in the hotel laundry, so he was sharp and freshly pressed in blue this morning.

Addison Walker had been true to his word, and the first paper had been delivered with coffee and pastries not long after dawn, giving Sasha time to read about himself in the newspaper.

It sounded so much more lurid than he remembered, but it would be an enormous rock landing in a mud puddle when the rest of America read it.

The Red Branch had arrived.

He had no idea what that implied, but he tucked his newspaper into a new suitcase, then answered the door carefully anyway, foot braced behind it and one hand ready for his pistol if something awkward or terrible was about to occur.

Two men in the hallway. Dark suits. Hats. Intense eyes.

"Sasha Kryvenko?" the shorter one asked in a quiet voice.

"That's right," Sasha replied.

The man reached inside his jacket and pulled out a wallet, flipping it open to show a badge and ID.

"Agent Donahue, sir," he said. "Federal Bureau of Investigation. My partner, Agent Baskins. We've been in touch with Sheriff Rogers and would like to take you into protective custody."

Sasha nodded.

This was that proverbial *other shoe dropping*.

"A moment?" he asked, waiting for them to nod and crossing to Lyuba's door to knock.

She answered immediately, so she was as anxious as he was, it seemed.

They shared a nod.

Sasha turned back and gestured the two men into his room. Lyuba brought the suitcase she had acquired yesterday and set it next to the matching one in his closet. The poor older gentleman at the store had had to call his wife to come up front and help with various feminine things that had also gotten packed, but he and Lyuba had left Paraguay in a hurry.

Inside, the door was closed and he moved to the table. Lyuba sat on the bed. Agent Baskins leaned against the wall. Agent Donahue sat across from Sasha.

"You have been briefed?" Sasha asked grimly.

Donahue took a long moment to study their uniforms.

"Possibly insufficiently, sir," he offered.

Sasha nodded. Details would have been lost in the long chain that had delivered these men to rural Virginia.

"*Banshee* can provide you all the technical details on the aircraft that your superiors will need," Sasha said, gesturing to her.

"*Banshee*?"

"We all fly under codenames," Sasha smiled. "They call me

Cernunnos, for the lord of the hunt in Irish mythology. She is *Banshee*. We left *Ecne* in Paraguay with the rest of the team."

"I see," Donahue nodded, still grim and a little lost from his eyes. Then he looked to the closet. "Are you prepared to depart for Washington, D.C.?"

"We are," Sasha replied. "Given enough time to review this mission, I do not believe that any other outcome is acceptable at this point, as there have been many things happening in the shadows that need to come out into the light."

He did not mention the newspaper. If they had missed what Mr. Walker had done overnight, it might be too late to stop that news from getting out later.

Sasha knew he was taking a risk, but the Red Branch would need to be on some sort of terms with the Americans after this. Better if they were friends. And not just their government.

All of them.

"We have a car downstairs," Donahue said. "We could immediately depart and get to D.C. by late afternoon, if you were prepared for a hard drive, sir."

"Whatever it takes, Agent Donahue," Sasha said, rising.

Whatever it took.

CHAPTER 55

Lyuba was seated in back of the sedan, next to Sasha, as the two American rode up front. She supposed that their Federal Bureau of Investigation was close enough to the Ministry of State Security back in Russia, though they did not give off the same energy of secret police. Or Gestapo.

Still, the air in the auto was brittle with emotions, even as lovely as the drive was. They had started early. Driven hard, as Agent Donahue had suggested, and eaten an early lunch in Richmond, the capital of Virginia, she thought.

Then another hard drive on roads and highways growing progressively busier, but they were approaching the American equivalent of Moscow. Perhaps more.

Brand new automobiles in all directions, mixing with older models that had been copied by the Soviet Union. Tall buildings in the distance, though this side of the river was still growing.

It did not take long to get there, once they hit the city limits. The highway seemed to aim straight at the building, then they dropped into a parking lot, then an underground parking garage guarded by grim-faced soldiers with weapons in hand. Donahue had to show papers to get in before they were allowed to pass.

Thus, they had arrived. Whatever was about to happen next. The Legion had been planning to drop bombs on the building yesterday.

Donahue parked in a spot and they were immediately met by more men, and a few soldiers who blanched at her pistol.

"Ma'am, you'll need to leave that outside," one of the soldiers informed her, pointing.

Several stripes on his sleeve, so a noncom. Not a man in charge, but a veteran soldier with opinions.

She looked at Sasha as he came around the rear of the car.

"Sergeant, who do we leave them with, that we'll get them back when we depart?" Sasha asked in that *Major Kryvenko* voice that had all the soldiers unconsciously snapping to. And the agents.

All of this presumed, of course, that they would be allowed to leave.

Did the Americans have an equivalent to Siberia for their exiles and prisoners? None that she was aware of, but history and geography were not her interests.

The sergeant glanced at one of the plainclothes secret police and got a nod.

"I'll take care of that, sir," he said. "Right this way."

Lyuba fell in on Sasha's flank like a wingman, surrounded by the others, as the sergeant led them to a small command post and pulled out a clipboard. He wrote several things, then tore the bottom half off and handed it to her as she cleared the Shanxi and placed it on the counter.

".45 ACP?" the man asked, leaning in but pointedly not touching the weapon.

"That is correct," Lyuba replied. "Shanxi Type 17. Manufactured originally by Chinese warlord Yan Xishan, who built a modern arms factory in his capital city of Taiyuan before the war. It allows us to use a Thompson .45 M1A1 while on the ground, without worrying about ammunition compatibility."

Another American who didn't think that women could be soldiers. Or pilots. Or engineers.

"Huh," was the only response.

Sasha placed his next to it, then they turned to Donahue. That one got them in motion, the soldiers left behind to deal with her pistol, and, perhaps, her perfume, left on them as a mark.

Americans needed to grow up, obviously.

Down several hallways, then an elevator ride up, followed by more hallways, then a room with a vast, square table, coffee stand, and many men, both in nicer suits and uniforms indicating higher rank. An even mix of green she knew and a light blue she thought might mean Air Forces. If she understood the American shoulder boards correctly, nobody at the table below the rank of colonel, with several generals in attendance.

Staff aides around the outside of the room were flunkies, just as in any military meeting. She had been in enough over the last few years.

Donahue got them coffee, then seated them at the table. It had all been fairly polite until now. She had still wondered if they were going to be thrown into an interrogation room with two way mirrors and handcuffs.

A man entered. Older, in a double-breasted suit, gray widow's peak, and one of those diagonal striped ties that seemed to indicate membership in some secret society. He spoke first. And did not introduce himself as he came to the head of the table and laid out several papers in front of him.

Lyuba did contain her smile when he reached out a hand

and touched a newspaper on his immediate right. She had her own copy of it. Except that this one appeared to say Washington Post across the top instead of Danville Beacon.

Had Addison Walker truly stolen a march on his own government? The man had intended to make a tremendous splash with the Red Branch, and had wisely left off most of the details of both the Werewolf Legion and the Silver Eagle, save vague hints about a shadowy organization trying to destroy the American way of life.

"Major Kryvenko," the gentleman began, nodding to Sasha next to her. "Captain Gradskaya. I've obviously read the paper this morning. And my people have spoken with Sheriff Rogers in Danville at length. Addison Walker is not far behind you in being brought to D.C., after this particular stunt. But the news is out. My people have reviewed the notes. I'd like you to start from the top and bring us up to date about the Werewolf Legion."

Sasha nodded. Then paused.

"We have been driving all day, and had lunch in Richmond," he said. "At some point, dinner would be useful, but I can start the briefing now, and carry on as long as you need."

"This is Doctor Ethan Voight," the man said, gesturing to a middle-aged man in an unfashionable suit, somewhat down the table. "He's my expert on aeronautics and rocketry, so he'll ask the technical questions. Brigadier General Carlyle is my military consultant. Major, how much of what you told Rogers and Walker is a complete pile of horseshit?"

Lyuba caught Sasha's grin.

"Very little of it, actually," Sasha replied, pausing to look around the wider table and catch eyes.

Lyuba noted four different people taking notes, either in

books or on some strange typewriter that only seemed to have a few keys.

"What I did—what we found necessary—was to only give Sheriff Rogers distinct pieces of the whole," Sasha continued. "Walker also had some of that, plus many of the extraneous details he wanted about our personal lives and how the Red Branch came into existence."

General Carlyle had a chest of medals and pins like a Soviet Marshal, lacking only the Stars.

"Ex-Soviet pilots?" Carlyle practically sneered. "Purged and exiled? Taken in by a group of Irish industrialists and given money, equipment, and whatever else? We're supposed to believe that?"

Lyuba allowed no reaction onto her face. There were armed guards around the outside walls as well.

"They call themselves Irish patriots, General," Sasha volleyed right back in the man's face. "Independent after the Revolution. And capitalists, because while the Red Branch is an expensive proposition to operate, it is also a highly profitable one. Many people think that guns are a satisfactory tool, when you need something violent done. They hardly ever consider that the skill and training of the man or woman holding the gun is even more important. The same goes for combat aircraft. My pilots and crew are all veterans of the Great Patriotic War. Captain Gradskaya flew with the Night Witches. The 46th **Guards** Night Bomber Aviation Regiment."

Lyuba smiled when the man turned and scowled at her. It would probably be rude to suggest that she had likely many times more combat experience and flight hours than the man in the pretty blue uniform with all the medals did. Possibly as much as ALL the pilots in her combined.

She considered it anyway.

The man in charge cracked a verbal whip before the General took more than a breath.

"Major, let us assume the Red Branch for now," he said. "Tell me about this Flying Wing you supposedly shot down in Argentina."

Lyuba sat back with her coffee and listened. Sasha could weave a mesmerizing tale when he chose to.

Their future lives probably depended on it.

Sasha studied the smaller table where they sat, in a commissary not far from the conference room where he had just spent several hours talking and answering questions. The hour was late, but the place was still buzzing with people.

General Carlyle was across from Lyuba and Dr. Voight sat across from him. Others filled in spaces on both sides working outwards.

Dinner was less appetizing than lunch, but still better than he usually got in a Soviet Red Air Forces mess hall. Several steps down from eating with General Navarro y Garcia at his palace, though. Still, an adequate roast beef, served open faced on bread, with potatoes.

"Blackhawks?" General Carlyle was asking Lyuba. "The Curtiss-Wright XF-87 that was prototyped but never built?"

"That is correct, General," she told him. "An interesting design, but not as effective as our Nightvipers, even improved as I suspect these were. Three of us took down four of them, before we went after the Wing."

Carlyle glanced at Sasha, but he nodded, backing his wing-woman entirely. And Vanya had actually taken on all four by himself before help could arrive. And gotten two kills.

"And the wreckage is still there?" the man pursued doggedly.

"I can provide you the vectors necessary to locate it," Sasha assured him. "Up in the mountains of Argentina, somewhere northwest of Cordoba, because they appeared to be flying a path where they would be over ocean as much as possible. Off the South American coast, across the Isthmus at Panama, possibly over Cuba, then up the American coast to New York City. General Navarro y Garcia should still have the footage of the various gun cameras in Argentina."

Dr. Voight cleared his throat and addressed Lyuba before the General could continue.

"And do we truly have flight vectors for the Silver Eagle?" Voight asked.

"Only roughly," Lyuba replied. "The heading was zero-six-zero true when we ejected. I had the autopilot forcing the nose to remain down, with the airbrakes fully deployed, but I have no way to determine how long those survived. My estimate would be a grid some two hundred kilometers long by perhaps fifty wide, if you were wishing to locate that wreckage. Could it be recovered?"

"Probably not, unless it landed in shallow enough waters on the continental shelf," Voight sighed. "At the same time, it it worth investigating, because obviously these people have solved some of the more intractable problems we are only now addressing."

Sasha nodded. The Legion had Gerstenberger, who might be a genius. And a psychopathic killer. Like Voss. They could afford to be a little reckless, if it only had to work once.

The General had finished eating last, mostly asking questions with a much less belligerent tone than before. Voight had asked most of them in the room. The one man in charge had listened to everything, only occasionally speaking.

An aide arrived and whispered in Carlyle's ear. Sasha pretended to ignore him and sipped some decaffeinated coffee.

"I've just been given word," Carlyle said after the aide stepped back. "It is late enough in the day that we'll break for now. Major, Captain, you'll be put up tonight in bachelor's quarters here. Obviously isolated from the general population, but I am at pains to inform you that you are not prisoners. The National Military Establishment is going to be busy, following up everything that has come to light in the last forty-eight hours. We appreciate that you have made yourselves available and answered all of our questions. If it would be acceptable, we're flying in some more experts from Texas that will arrive overnight, and we'd like to spend a week fully debriefing you on things."

"I need to get a message to my people in Dublin, General," Sasha replied. "They'll be in touch with my various forward teams in South America as soon as possible. After that, we'll work with your people, but I will remind you that we are mercenary contractors. My company has completed the current job and I will need to be looking for our next employer shortly."

Carlyle's eyes got a twinkle in them that Sasha didn't necessarily trust, but was in no position to argue. Not while surrounded by agents and soldiers, in the middle of the entire American war apparatus.

Still, the man rose, smiling. Sasha joined him, as did the rest of the table. Obviously, things had reached a turning point.

Sasha assumed that everyone else would return to the conference room and spend a good portion of the evening arguing. Or leaving their staff to produce various reports that could be delivered on.

He wasn't entirely certain how their bureaucracy worked, save that it tended to be a giant steamroller. You got out of the way when it was moving, or got crushed.

"The captain here will see you to quarters," Carlyle told them. "I will see you in the morning."

Then they were alone, with a nervous captain in a lighter blue uniform, as everyone else silently filed out. Back to work.

Sasha let the man lead them deeper into the complex. Eventually, they ended up in a dead-end corridor, where the rooms appeared to be of a type where senior officers were assigned. Certainly luxurious and spacey, with his own private bath and shower, instead of sharing with others communally.

Lyuba was in the next room, and both had their suitcases. He supposed that at some point, laundry would be a problem, but he had civilian clothing he could wear for now.

And maybe he would convince Gennadi to send more uniforms when he sent a cable.

How deep into his new role was he about to fall, like Alice finding a rabbit hole?

Sasha had no idea.

And no way out.

CHAPTER 57

Sasha wore a simple brown suit. Off the rack, but a close enough fit. Better fit than anything he had worn before. And a better fabric, but he had never been a clothes horse.

Merely a pilot, trying to do the best he could.

An Air Force sergeant was assigned as an aide, taking his uniform for laundry and inquiring about his needs. Lyuba had a stern-faced woman in civilian gear as well.

To go with his suit, Lyuba wore slacks and a tunic that got many scowls from the men around them, but he knew how immune she was as she scowled back.

They had spoken only briefly last night, assuming someone listening. Mostly reassuring each other that all was well, and that they would make it out the far side of this.

Sasha still didn't know how.

But the same captain from last night had escorted them to breakfast, then the conference room, still filled with cigarette smoke, though someone had cleaned up the coffee, ashtrays, and other detritus from yesterday.

Several new faces this morning. Some of the men from yesterday were absent, including the FBI men.

Sasha didn't know what to make of that, other than it seemed a positive development.

The same nameless man in charge. Still perfectly presented, though a different suit and tie today. The same hawk-like visage, watching everything with hungry eyes.

"Major Kryvenko, this is Dr. Xaver Hummel," he introduced the one who seemed in charge of the new group.

Sasha had to still any reaction before it made it to his eyes, because on paper, he should have no idea who the man was. Wouldn't know that he had been one of von Braun's top people at Peenemünde. Didn't know that Hummel been one of the ones responsible for the slave labor that had built their rocket base, at a cost of their lives, executed either during or after, as secrets had to be protected.

Sasha calmly shook hands with the devil himself, then sat back down in the same chair as yesterday.

"I've been briefed," Hummel told him in a thin German accent as everyone else settled. "I have several questions on the Silver Eagle aircraft."

"Then you should be talking to *Banshee*," Sasha smiled cruelly at the man as he nodded to Lyuba, watching Hummel swallow his distaste.

Another Nazi *Übermenschen* who thought that women belonged in the kitchen or bedroom, from the look in the man's eyes.

Lyuba perked up. She was already driving the men in here a bit mad by not dressing as a housewife or secretary. And the slacks she had chosen had did not hug her curves in ways that might suggest a dancer or sex object.

"How may I assist, Dr. Hummel?" she asked in an equally polite and emotionless voice that was perhaps all the more cruel for lacking any sort of implied superiority beyond her mere words.

But then, Sasha already knew how many fools underestimated that woman. And had watched her shoot them all down.

Literally, even.

Hummel gulped, swallowing whatever pique he might have brought up, then settled and began asking questions. Hard ones. Technical ones.

Sasha was lost by the third sentence. Looking around, three-quarters of the men in here—and they were all men save Lyuba—were as well, so he didn't feel as bad.

He instead presumed victory in a game he could not even score adequately, since Lyuba's voice never went past conversational, even at one point where Voight and Hummel were practically screaming at one another and Sasha thought that they might come to blows before the nameless man cracked his whip on them again.

The morning session went fast. That was well, as Lyuba simply upset their male superiority with her calm assuredness. Sasha answered the few questions sent his way as her back-seat flight engineer, but she had been in control from the moment they had closed the canopy.

She had gotten them here.

And, judging by eyes, many of the military pilots around the table were a bit in awe of the woman.

Sasha welcomed the company.

Lunch again, in the same place. General Carlyle joined them, but not Dr. Voight. There might be more screaming behind closed doors. And suggestions to the navy to go find the wreckage by hook or by crook, since Lyuba had provided her vectors and estimates.

He'd have expected a smaller box to search in, but nobody knew how the plane would fly once they ejected and changed all the aerodynamics. And maybe she didn't want it found.

It had not exploded before he had bailed out. That was sometimes as good as you were going to get.

"Major, I have a question for you," Carlyle said as they finished up eating, glancing at Lyuba to include her in the conversation, but maintaining his focus forward.

"Go on," Sasha replied, noting that the three of them were alone at this table today, where it had been a dozen last night.

"You mentioned previously that your contract with Mr. Hernandez might have concluded, as he had tasked you with investigating a communist insurrection threat to his organization, and that had led you to the Legion base," Carlyle continued. "Do I have that correct?"

It had been the best lie Sasha and Gennadi had been able to come up with that covered attacking a Paraguayan air force base. And Hernandez knew that they were stalking the Legion. He had hired them specifically for that reason on the General's request, though Sasha imagined that he might have gotten some bombing practice in the brush, had Voss's Legion not been building another superweapon.

There probably was rebellion in the woods, but likely no more than villagers brutalized by the elite power structure and willing to accept arms and assistance from anyone wanting to throw down hereditary aristocracy and kulaks.

Sasha would have helped, right up until the moment that Colonel Nazarenko had walked up to the bars of his cell and offered him an entirely different fate in life.

"That is correct, General," He nodded. "Hernandez feared new aircraft in the hands of another, inimical private mercenary company such as ours, which was why he reached out to General Navarro y Garcia to hire us."

"There are brush wars going on in Central and South America," Carlyle agreed. "Before and during the war. The peace has not slowed them one bit. Do you expect more mercenaries?"

"The world is awash in arms, General," Lyuba chimed in. "The American government saw itself as the arsenal of democracy, and provided weapons to anyone friendly. More are available everywhere now that the fighting is over. In our case, a few aircraft and expert pilots can make all the difference in the world. And have, as you've seen."

Carlyle had been converted to her side. Sasha had watched it occur as she had held her own with all the men who thought themselves experts on the topic. His nod was respectful today.

Sasha watched the man come to some internal decision. The light in his eyes changed.

Not bad, but surreptitious, perhaps.

"If the Red Branch was available and seeking employment, would you object to being quietly approached by certain elements of the American government?" Carlyle asked quietly.

Sasha nearly dropped his coffee, but managed to remain cool on the outside.

"To what purpose, General?" he asked carefully, aware that there was nobody else close enough to overhear this conversation, even inside the depths of the Pentagon, itself a secured fortress with layers of protection in place.

"The Werewolf Legion has, by your account, attempted to attack the United States twice in the last year or so," Carlyle said. "Only your luck in being able to stop them has presumably kept bombs from falling on New York City or Washington, D.C., Sasha."

Sasha noted that the man had stopped calling him *Major Kryvenko*.

He nodded. Everything he and Lyuba had told these people could be validated independently. Perhaps had, if they had had time to reach out to the General, or his people. Or had spies in South America reporting home regularly.

Gennadi's cover in Dublin would be tested, but the Irish had a wariness about dealing with friends of the British, in spite of old ties of blood to America. And the folks that had been brought in in Ireland were all solid Republicans with at least *Fuchsia* Catholic Socialist tendencies, rather than *Orange* Protestant Capitalists.

There would be another guerrilla war on that island at some point, seeking to finally unify it, but Sasha didn't think that would happen yet. Only after England weakened to the point that their empire decayed. Perhaps not even then. Time would tell.

"You would have us hunt the Legion directly?" Sasha asked the man point-blank.

"Not necessarily directly, no," Carlyle shook his head and dropped his voice. "But you have been conducting certain operations in Argentina that we have become aware of since looking closer."

Such as, overnight, someone had asked their spies for input, and possibly even listened to them.

"Go on," Sasha prodded the man.

"We would like to hire you for certain tasks," Carlyle nodded. "Perhaps provide upgrade your equipment, since the Vampire is an older model and we are producing far better aircraft today."

Sasha held up one finger to stop the man there. Watched this Air Force General stop expectantly.

"The Nightviper we fly today is possibly as good as anything you have, General," he said quietly. "Our friends have radically upgraded the platform. I flew early MiG-15s as a test pilot before all this. The skill of the pilot would be the difference against my Nightvipers, not the aircraft itself."

Carlyle's eyes got huge. But Sasha knew that the Americans would demand to know more about his planes if they were to hire him. And the new MiGs, if he was available to answer questions they would have. And he was not a spy for anyone, but he could say certain things.

If the Americans thought that the Soviet Air Forces had quality aircraft equal to theirs, they might be less inclined to start a war.

Because the MiG-15 really was a revolution on wings. It had better maneuverability at high altitude and speed than the Nightviper, but not much.

Down low, he would dogfight anybody.

Carlyle remained silent an extra moment.

"Three of us shot down four upgraded Blackhawks, General," Lyuba reminded the man. "Plus, the Nightviper is an all-weather interceptor and attack craft. I am not aware of anything you are building of a comparable role at the moment. Your night-fighters are all older propeller craft. Your Shooting Stars and Panthers are not as good in the attack role. Nor as good as the Nightviper to dogfight."

Carlyle blinked at her, then remembered that she might be smarter than he was and closed his mouth, words unspoken.

Sasha waited another beat, then smiled to take the sting out of his words.

Right here, right now, was an outcome beyond Gennadi's wildest dreams, if it put the Red Branch in a position to be paid by the Americans to kill war criminals.

And keep the global peace.

"We are probably looking for work, General," Sasha nodded intently. "What sort of contract might be on tender?"

He sat back and let the man talk.

What could he accomplish with American backing, too?

CHAPTER 58

Sasha popped the canopy on Red-1 as he came to rest, surrounded by American airmen in blue bringing him and the others on the side of the runway where his four Nightvipers would be stored for now, with Yuri's camel Verblyud already on the end.

Yanina had ferried Red-4. And done a credible job of it, but Sasha knew that he would need a fourth pilot soon. These craft required two-person crews. One to fly. One to operate the radar systems that made them so deadly in the dark.

Around them, an American air base, with a long row of Lockheed P-80 Shooting Stars. In a hangar nearly, the newer North American F-86 Sabre. Two rows of them under cover.

Sasha exited, gathering up his team as the ground crews went to work chocking things and making sure the aircraft were secured. Yuri would supervise, but everything had gotten a good round of maintenance before leaving home, and it had been a clean ferry flight, to a space in Nevada where they had landed today. The middle of nowhere, surrounded by desert.

A staff car and several trucks were arriving nearby. Brigadier General Carlyle emerged in his blue uniform. Sasha made his way over to the man, Lyuba and Vanya accompanying on his wings.

"*Cernunnos*, thank you for coming," Carlyle said as they got close.

Sasha shook his hand, as did the other two. Carlyle was even treating Lyuba like a fighter pilot today, rather than a woman who had wandered along.

It was good. The man had power and connections that Sasha sought to exploit.

"Thank you for inviting us, General," Sasha replied.

"I have the trucks for your people, Sasha," Carlyle said, "but I wanted to take the three of you over to see our newest interceptor. A day fighter, obviously, but one we find highly advanced. I'd like you to compare it to other aircraft you have flown."

He began to walk towards the hangar without looking back. Vanya had a surprised look. Lyuba was calm and smiling.

Sasha led.

The first thing that struck him about the F-86 was the length. At least one third-again longer than the MiG-15 on first glance, but otherwise, remarkably similar. Slight barrel shaped to the body. Air intakes on the nose. Low, swept wings.

The tail was the big visual difference. The MiG-15 had a T-shaped tail, with the horizontal stabilizers high, while the Sabre had them down at the base of the vertical stabilizer. He wasn't sure if that would improve aerodynamics at mach-approaching speeds, which generally seemed to be the latest problem to solve with the MiG.

Not that he would tell the Americans that. At least not yet.

Remarkably similar aircraft, though. Cousins, one might call them, at least externally.

Carlyle had come to rest, so Sasha joined him, with Vanya outside the General's arm and Lyuba outside his.

"I can point out the obvious visual differences, General," Sasha said. "Without flying one, however, there it not much I can say."

"That's why we're here, Major," General Carlyle said. "I've gotten clearance from my people to have you, Captain Gradskaya, and Captain Zhidkov trained on flying the new Sabrejets we're in the process of turning operational with our squadrons."

"Sir?" Sasha asked, confused, elated, concerned, and wary all at once.

"It might be possible to refit the Red Branch with Sabres, Sasha," Carlyle turned and smiled. "Or we might want to look at how your Nightviper design could be improved."

"Swept wings is an obvious modification," Lyuba offered. "Perhaps twin-engine, since we already have the width with side-by-side seating, so that could improve our power."

"Exactly, Captain," Carlyle said. "You personally impressed the shit out of a lot of Air Force people, back in Washington. While we're hunting down the Werewolf Legion, we'd like to take advantage of the combined expertise your force represents, to see how we could do things better."

"And would we be allowed to transfer technology to our own factory, back in Ireland?" Sasha asked, thrilled with the prospect that Gennadi might make better Nightvipers. "To upgrade our craft?"

Or keep the Soviet Air Forces on the same cutting edge as the Americans, if a war ended up being inevitable.

The Nazis had had better aircraft from Day One. Only quantity had kept them in check.

Quantity of blood spilled.

"That's being discussed at the highest levels right now, Major," Carlyle nodded, taking Sasha's breath away with the ramifications. "We'll need to meet with your White Russian boss and take his measure, obviously, but you've earned a lot of goodwill with the politicians looking for a public, political win after it looks like China is a lost cause."

Sasha could have told them that. Chiang Kai-Shek had, from what he'd been told, always been a fantastic politician and an asshole of a person. And a jealous general, forever destroying any of his subordinates who might somehow threaten his power by being better commanders. Even when such actions left him weaker in the face of Comrade Mao's disciplined troops.

Endgame was almost upon China. They had lost the north last year. They had lost the center over the summer. Only a few holdouts in the south remained, but the Nationalists had already mostly fled to Formosa.

Good riddance to them.

"So you want us to fly Sabres for a time, General?" Sasha asked, pointedly and perhaps legally.

"Yes," Carlyle replied, turning to face him. "That, and keep saving the world."

Sasha nodded.

That much he could promise.

READ MORE!

Be sure to pick up all the books in The Red Branch series!
https://www.knottedroadpress.com/series/the-red-branch

ABOUT THE AUTHOR

Blaze Ward writes science fiction in the Alexandria Station universe (Jessica Keller, The Science Officer, Phil Kosnett, etc.) as well as several other science fiction universes, such as Corsac Fox, Operation Marrakesh, and more. In addition, he is the Editor and Publisher of *Boundary Shock Quarterly Magazine as well as Thrill Ride Magazine* . You can find out more at his website www.blazeward.com, as well as Patreon, bluesky, Facebook, Goodreads, and other places.

Blaze's works are available as ebooks, paper, and audio, and can be found at a variety of online vendors. His newsletter comes out regularly, and you can also follow his blog on his website. He really enjoys interacting with fans, and looks forward to any and all questions—even ones about his books!

Never miss a release!

If you'd like to be notified of new releases, sign up for my newsletter.

http://www.blazeward.com/newsletter/

Buy More!

Did you know that you can buy directly from the KRP website?

ABOUT KNOTTED ROAD PRESS

Knotted Road Press publishes dynamic fiction set in exotic locations and unique non-fiction voices in genres such as autobiography, business, cookbooks, and how-to. Our authors cover a wide range of genres including science fiction, fantasy, mystery, literary, and poetry, appealing to all readers. We offer both DRM-free ebooks and print books for a global readership.

Knotted Road Press
www.KnottedRoadPress.com
www.KnottedRoadPress.com/Shop

www.ingramcontent.com/pod-product-compliance
Lightning Source LLC
Chambersburg PA
CBHW070517100726
47907CB00004B/880